THE NAKED PLANT

The Naked Plant

H. L. Wickins

The Pentland Press Limited
Edinburgh Cambridge Durham

British Library Cataloguing in Publication Data

This novel is a work of fiction and based loosely on the author's childhood. Names, characters, places and incidents are the product of the author's imagination. Any resemblance to actual persons, living or dead, is entirely coincidental.

ISBN 1 872795 40 4

Typeset in 10pt Times by
Print Origination, (NW) Ltd., Formby, Liverpool L37 8EG

About the author

The author, born in 1913, the youngest of four brothers, was educated at the Reading Blue Coat School and went on to qualify as a Chartered Surveyor in Valuation. During the war he saw service in India, the Middle East and Burma. He also began his writing career at that time and had several short stories published in Forces magazines. He is a member of the Civil Service Authors and the Penman Club. On his retirement in 1973 he went to live in Wales.

This is H. L. Wickins' first novel in a saga of the twentieth century.

Acknowledgements

The author wishes to acknowledge the following sources, which provided invaluable background information in the writing of *The Naked Plant:*
Edmond, *Official History of the War;* Bryon Farwell, *The Great Boer War;* James Joyce, *Ulysses;* John Wittow, *Disasters;* I F Grant, *The Clan Grant;* John Richard Green, *A Short History of the English People;* The Jersey Evening Post; The Reading Standard; The Oxford University Press; *The Oxford Dictionary of Quotations.*

For my mother

The lopped tree in time may grow again;
Most naked plants renew both fruit and flower;
From *Times go by Turns* by Robert Southwell

Chapter 1

Nell Sedgewick, small and slim, aproned, her sleeves rolled up to the elbows, opened the piano, flicked the notes with her duster and ascended the scale, fast and furiously, from the lowest to the topmost ivory of the keyboard. On a ladder to heaven, her spirits soared. News from France was good. The Allies were on the march. She had a feeling of optimism. Soon, the war would be over. When Jack came home she would be ready for him. The sun flooded the little front room and made all the furniture look polished and shining. Lucky Jack. That's what the recruiting sergeant had called him. His brother and sister, Alf and Lyd, had told her the story many times. Now, giving everything an extra rub with her rag, she remembered and chuckled to herself.

Alf and Lyd never wanted their brother to be a soldier. Lyd blamed Queen Victoria. Alf blamed the recruiting sergeant. They were orphans, looked after by an aunt, a tartar who could not get rid of them quick enough. When Alf got a job at the brewery stables she complained of the smell, so he left her and went into lodgings. Soon afterwards, Lyd went into service. That left Jack, short and stocky, who, at the Diamond Jubilee, stretched tall to see the Great White Mother, the only one he had, as she passed the cheering crowd. Dazzled by flags, red uniforms, brass bands, he told his brother and sister he wanted to be a soldier. Alf told him not to be so daft. Lyd said, if he wanted to go upstairs with his brains blown out, that was up to him, but, when she died, she wanted to lay her down in the peace and quiet of her own land, not some jungle with lions and tigers roaring and snarling over her, nor some desert with vultures picking her bones, nor some mountain with ice and snow for her last resting place.

Nell, kind eyed and gentle, thought the same as her sister-in-law about soldiering. She would never have chosen to marry a soldier, but had not been able to help herself. Just for a moment, the way she sometimes prayed, she sat down with the rag on her lap and looked at the framed enlargement of their last photograph together, with Jack a sergeant in khaki. Nell enjoyed such quiet moments, her four boys out of the house, and she alone, thinking about her husband. The sunlight from the window opposite showed up a smear on the glass, so she stood on the maroon rexine cover of the chair and wiped it clean.

Nell left the front room and went into the scullery to peel potatoes for the midday meal. She giggled again as she recalled the rest of the story of Jack's recruitment. He would not listen to his brother and sister. He wanted to make his way in the world, as they were doing. His aunt encouraged him.

'Grow great in fame,' she said, 'be the arm of the Queen.'

So he went to the barracks. Alf and Lyd, believing he would be turned down, went with him. They were not surprised when the sergeant, fat as a pig, when he saw young Jack, no bigger than a threepenny bit, laughed red behind the spikes of his moustache, and shake like a jelly under his red tunic. But they were worried when the sergeant told their brother not to worry about being small, "cos it's the fat ones as cops it. As long as you're brave,' he said, 'like Joan o'Marble Arch, the Maid o' HORleans, an' BOWdacea, an' Mary Ambree foremost in the battle, an' Rule Brittania wiv 'er shield an' spear. All women, was't they? An' ain't you brave as any woman?'

Lyd told Nell that she knew she had a fight on her hands when she saw Jack stick out his chest to show how brave he was, and the sergeant told him he had to have ambition. No good being a private and being bawled at all your life. See the world the easy way, like him. He'd been all over: Gib., Africa, Injia, China. Followed the sun like a dog. Done a bit up the Kyber. Fired a few shots. Kept out of trouble. Buried a few comrades. Lucknow was the worst. Injian Mutiny. Women and children cut to pieces. Officers blowing their bleeding brains out. All over a bit of pig's fat. Funny lot, them Injians, worshipping them cows and queer looking fellows with all of them arms and legs and heads. Brahmer Creator. Vishner Preserver. Shiver Destroyer. Hundreds of them. He never did sort them all out. Too much creating and destroying, and not enough preserving in Injia. Millions died of famine and pestilence. Rajputana, Orissa, Madras, Bombay. Vultures tearing up corpses. 'All 'cos their gawd an' preserver sent no rain an' fried 'em all up in the sun. An' they talks abaht the murderin' British soldier. I asks yer.'

Nell smiled to herself when she pictured Jack gaping open mouthed like a fish and taking it all in. It was just what he wanted, to be like the sergeant, with his own wide knowledge of the world.

The sergeant finally hooked young Jack. 'You're an orphan, ain't you? Jack Sedgeman, ain't you?' he asked.

'Sedgewick, sir,' Jack said.

'Same fing, ain't it?' said the sergeant, 'An' gawd 'elps orphins, don't 'e? An' gawd keeps watch for the life o' young Jack, Ain't you Jack the orphin? Nothin's goin' to 'arm an orphin the name o' Jack.'

Fighting for the body and soul of her brother, Lyd asked what about Ben Battle, the soldier bold, and used to wars alarms, but a cannon ball shot off his legs, so he laid down his arms? She told Jack not to listen to the sergeant, because soldiers were a lying, drunken, vicious lot of men, and not to be trusted. The sergeant only laughed. 'None o' that sort o' language 'ere my gal,' he said.

Alf and Lyd argued with their brother all the way home, but Jack, stubborn as a mule, had made up his mind, so off he went and joined the Surreys. Soon, he was off to fight the Boers, not yet twenty.

Jack had told her all about that, too. General Buller making them all eat a hot meal every day in the blazing sun; and the cavalry officer who wore gold spurs. At the Battle of Colenso twenty thousand men marched in the red dust to fight the Boers in the kopjes the other side of the Tugela River – 'The Terrible One'. General Hildyard ordered the Surreys, the Devons, the Queens and West Yorks to advance swiftly in extended lines. With mausers firing, and Lyddite shells bursting yellowish green, Jack remembered his sergeant shouting

'Now, lads, you ain't 'ere to go to sleep an' dream of 'ome. Keep yer bladdy 'eads dahn an' yer bleedin' eyes open, an' its gawd 'elp the one I sees wiv a bullet in 'is back.'

The man from *The Daily Telegraph* said they were a superb spectacle of invincible manhood. The Surreys got to the bridge, and some of the other troops were halfway up Shwangwahnee Hill on the other side of the river. Bugler Dunn, a boy in the Dublin Fusiliers, disobeyed orders, stayed at the front, took it into his head to sound the advance, and sent men plunging to death in the Tugela River – 'The Terrible One'. Then Colonel Long lost his guns, so General Buller brought back all his men to Frere where they started out in the morning. After the battle, a mad

English officer went wandering amongst the dead and wounded. Vultures snatched at the meat wrapped up in khaki drill. Bugler Dunn came home a hero and had an audience with the Queen.

Mrs. Stevens, Nell's next door neighbour, called from over the fence at the back. 'Can I come in?'

Nell went to the back door and said, 'Yes. Come and have a cup of tea.' She put the kettle on, then peeled the last potato and dropped it like a bomb into the saucepan.

Mrs. Stevens, a tall, amiable woman who bullied her husband, a compulsive gambler half her size, occasionally shared a pot of tea or a jug of stout with Nell. Rosie, her youngest girl, was teaching David, Nell's youngest, a five-year-old, to ride her bike. She rushed along the street, dumped the old bike on the asphalt pavement outside her house, and rushed indoors to the outside lavatory. David followed her. 'Let's play Adam and Eve,' Rosie said, transforming the smelly place into Paradise before the Fall, and let down her drawers. David dropped his trousers. Mrs. Stevens, when she walked past the loo to call Nell, caught the two of them at it. She told Nell all about it over a cup of tea. 'The little hussy,' she said. 'leading your baby astray.'

The women laughed.

'Soon, he'll have his daddy to play with him,' Nell said.

'This bloody war,' said Mrs. Stevens. 'It's got to end soon.'

'Jack is lucky,' Nell said. 'He survived the Boer War. It looks as though he will survive this one.'

In the afternoon the telegraph boy, who had lost himself in a criss-cross of terraces, finally turned into Cheese Row, stopped at Nell's house, parked his bicycle on the kerb and knocked at the door. David, playing hop-scotch on the pavement with the girls, left the game and rushed indoors to tell his mother, busy in the scullery.

'It's a telegraph boy,' David said.

Nell sat on a stool in her kitchen and read the telegram. David, always nearest her lap, perched on her knee. They were alone in the house. Nell resisted as long as she could, but, when the pressure became too great, her eyes filled, and she asked David to go outside and play.

For many days and nights, except in periods of complete numbness of thought and feeling, a flotsam and jetsam of happy and bitter memories flooded in on a tide of tears. At such moments she felt like a casualty of some natural disaster; a drowning woman carried away and submerged in the waters of a rainstorm perhaps, or a tidal wave. All her life appeared before her; scraps of reality gathered hurriedly for instant despatch to God knows what depths of darkness or oblivion.

Her family had never wanted her to marry Jack. Nell remembered the first day they met, when she and Miss Alice, to whom she was nursemaid, came back from having their photo taken in Richmond, and found Jack at the gate of the big house in St. Margaret's Road. There he was, Corporal Jack Sedgewick, in red tunic, stripes and medal, waiting for his sister Lyd who worked in the kitchen, to take her out for the afternoon. Lyd persuaded Nell to go with them.

In Richmond Park, near Kidney Wood, they sat on the dry grass and argued about peace and war. On that hot, summer day Jack lay prone, the top buttons of his tunic undone, chewing a dry stalk and looking into the sky. 'Someone has to fight the country's wars,' he said, more seriously than Nell expected. He told her he had three more years to go. 'Will you wait for me?' he asked. Lyd told him not to be cheeky, and mind his manners, but could not keep a straight face. Jack got up on his elbows and searched out all Nell's secrets. She felt an irrepressible force invading and overwhelming her. He would be what he wished and win what he desired. It frightened her. Her only escape was in silence, so she allowed Jack and Lyd to talk out the afternoon until she was free again; alone and free in thought either to encourage or deny his power.

Her boys dragged her back into the real world. George, the eldest, then Andrew and Pat, then David, born a year before the start of this terrible war. It had been Jack's idea to name his sons after the patron saints of the United Kingdom with an Empire on which the sun never set.

David and Pat came in quarrelling.

'Go outside if you want to fight,' she said, and turned them out.

Nell could not help thinking of what had been and what might have been. 'If only,' she said to herself many times, 'but still,' she said, and relived joys again. 'Happy the wooing that's not long adoing,' she wrote on her postcard to him, and, six months after that first meeting in Richmond Park, she crossed the Channel and married him in St. Helier on the Island of Jersey. No family. Just her and Jack and two of his comrades, one his best man, the other to give her away.

Now he was dead. She could not change that. Did it matter that he had joined the army so young? Did it matter that, as a regular soldier, he had been recalled to his regiment at the beginning of the war? He might have been killed anyway. There had been millions of them. Some reservists like Jack, and others just civilians dressed for war.

The postman knocked.

'Go and see what he's brought,' said Nell, ironing, to George, helping her fold the sheets.

The boy rushed to the door and brought back a letter from the parish priest, who signed himself 'pastor and friend'. His message of condolence, printed on a stiff, white card, read

'God knows all, and He has not allowed this trouble to come to you without purpose of love in it. God has thought it all out beforehand, knowing what was best.'

The crossed flags at the top of the card had the inscription His banner over you is love. Nell put the card aside and finished her ironing. After a few days, when alone, she looked at the card again and repeated the inscription to herself. 'His banner over you is love'. She wondered where the text came from, and searched until she found it in *The Song of Solomon*. 'Let him kiss me with the kisses of his mouth: for thy love is better than wine . . .

'. . . I am the rose of Sharon, and the lily of the valleys.
    As the lily among thorns, so is my love among the daughters.
    As the apple tree among the trees of the wood, so is my beloved among the sons.
    I sat down under his shadow with great delight, and his fruit was sweet to my taste.
    He brought me to the banqueting house, and *his banner over me was love.*
    Stay me with flagons, comfort me with apples; for I am sick of love.
    His left hand is under my head, and his right hand doth embrace me.
    I charge you, O ye daughters of Jerusalem, by the roes, and by the hinds of the field, that ye stir not up, nor awake my love, till he pleases'

Struggling in the depths of her sorrow, Nell could not cope with the bitter irony of the message, nor the unexpected eroticism in sacred scripture. She herself had known that kind of love. Instead of giving her hope for the future, the poem of the Shulamite woman reminded her of what she had lost, and so added to her grief.

Jack liked the girls. Lyd had told her how much she worried about him when he first joined up, so young and green, like a little tin soldier in a bit of fresh paint, easy for the girls, with their pretty giggles and a kiss or two on the cheek, to stand him up and push him over and leave him around chipped and broken. The sergeant badgered him to find a girl to keep him on the straight and narrow. He told his sister he would like a girl to kiss, but she told him to take care and not be in too much hurry, and keep away from the bad girls and be a good boy. He told Lyd she did not have to worry. He had seen those naughty girls on picture postcards, with thighs like lace pillows, and their legs in black stockings with pink garters, and their titties falling out. They were not for him, he said. He wanted someone kind and gentle, just like her. Lyd told Nell that she could have eaten him for saying that.

Then he fell in love with Miss Celia, his 'Apple Blossom Girl'. It happened on the day he went to the big house in St. Margaret's Road to say goodbye to Lyd before he went to South Africa. In the drive he met Sir Humphrey, master of the house, with his daughter Miss Celia on his arm. Jack was worried about getting his sister into trouble with the master, who was strict about callers, but Miss Celia piped up and told her father who he was, and that he was going off to South Africa to fight the Boers. Lyd liked Miss Celia because she was a girl you could talk to, and she had told her about Jack coming to say goodbye. Sir Humphrey, dressed in black, his topper bright as a helmet, shoes shining like spurs, raised his stick with a silver knob, tapped Jack on the breast, said the Boers were wild animals, and it was lucky the country had such fine specimens of manhood to protect it, and the gold would make England the richest country on earth, and Jack would come home a hero and take any girl he wanted. Pretty Miss Celia, all in pink and white, looked embarrassed and stared at the ground, but when her father stopped talking, she looked up and laughed and told him not to be a summer soldier, a sunshine patriot. When she offered her hand to Jack to say goodbye and wish him luck, she pressed her thumb a bit harder and longer than she need have done, just to tell him she really meant it. Jack fell in love with her on the spot. His 'Apple Blossom Girl' he called her, and told Lyd that all he wanted was to get back safe and take Miss Celia for his sweetheart.

Poor Jack, thought Nell, and did not know whether to laugh or cry at the memory of it all. When he came back from the war and found Miss Celia married, he cursed Sir Humphrey for making promises which had not come true. Then his Great White Mother died, and he drowned his sorrows at the bar. Lyd started to worry about him again, drinking to quench his bitterness, and, on leave from Dublin's fair city where the girls are so pretty, joking with his comrades about a woman called Molly Bloom who liked the Surreys because every time she passed the men's

greenhouse near the Harcourt Street station, one of them tried to show it
to her, as though it was one of the Seven Wonders of the World. Then the
regiment moved to Jersey, and Lyd worried because that was where that
water Lily Langtree came from.

Nell laughed at the memory of Lyd Sedgewick and her stories, and it
lightened her burden. 'He's a good boy, really,' she used to tell Nell.
'Not a bit like a common soldier. You'd like him. What he needs is a wife
and family, not that silly old regiment he's so proud of. He's got some
leave this summer. Perhaps you'll meet him.' And Lyd took good care
that Nell did meet him at the gate when she and Miss Alice came back
from the photographers, by keeping Jack waiting until they arrived.

Nell had always suspected Lyd of arranging things, and she was glad.
Her thoughts turned back to her wedding day. After the ceremony Jack
took her on the train to St. Brelades. In the spring sunshine they sat on
the silver sand against the high sea wall of the bay between the quarry at
L'Ouaisne and the church at Beauport. Jack, a bit of a poet, loved the
little church under the trees where, he said, the gravestones slept on the
hill like sheep in the fold. Their first child would be christened there, he
said. They would also have lots of children and live to be a hundred.
After laughing and kissing away the afternoon, they had tea and bought
an *Evening Post* and read it under the palms. They laughed at the
American who planned to build a three million dollar bungalow with
gold walls and furniture, carpets and curtains made of yellow dollar bills,
and a Monte Carlo room for the servants.

Nell, forgetting her grief, smiled at that and other things in the
newspaper which had amused them. Jack wanted her to take him to the
Grand Corset Demonstration at Voisin & Co. There was a report of
another wedding that day, at St. Mark's. Society people with carriages, a
red carpet, a church full of flowers, the bride in a white methune Empire
gown with a train, the bridesmaids in mousseline de sois, and an organist
to play *The Wedding March*. At The Royal Hotel there was a reception
for seventy guests from all ranks of society. And there they were, they
laughed, with only a newspaper to amuse them.

They took the train back to St. Helier and saw *The Girl from Kay's* at
the Opera House, early door, for 1/6d in the Pit. Then they went back to
her room in Val Plaissant, and Jack told her about his 'Apple Blossom
Girl' because he wanted to get it off his chest before their wedding night.
And Nell told him he need not have bothered because Lyd had told her
already. So they laughed and then loved for the first time. 'Let him kiss

me with the kisses of his mouth; for thy love is better than wine,' she recited to herself, because that was how she remembered her wedding night, and Sunday too, the following day, until Jack went back to barracks in the evening.

Neighbours called; Mrs. Stevens next door, and others further down the street. Mrs. Titcombe, a grim, red-faced ogre, softened her expression for Nell. 'I'm so sorry,' she said. 'Is there anything I can do?' She had a street lamp outside her door. According to the season of the year, children used it as a goal-post for football, a wicket for cricket, tying ropes for skipping games, and as a prop for the first bent back in 'Puff Coming'. Andrew Sedgewick, for a dare, had swung on the ladder rest and broke his wrist. After dark, older boys used the lamp post as a base for 'Release', a rough war game based on the rescue of British prisoners from the Germans. The lamp attracted every noisy rabble to Mrs. Titcombe's door. No wonder she was bad tempered. Night and day she shouted at kids to go away, but to Nell she was kind.

Mrs. Cotterell, a plump, good humoured cockney, came to Nell's door with a jug of stout from the off-licence. 'Let's have a drink,' she said. Forget your troubles.' Her husband, slow and silent, spick and span in dark clothes, travelled to London every day with a black brief-case and umbrella. He was a mystery man, out of place in Cheese Row, and out of character with his rough and tumble family. Charley, the only boy, a suet pudding called 'Fatty' enjoyed practical jokes. He played with smaller children because boys his own age made fun of him. One day he asked young David Sedgewick into his house. They played leap frog. Charley knelt down, rested his head in his arms on the seat of a chair, but moved away when David leaped on him. David split his chin on the edge of the chair. Charley roared. Nell came, and led David away bleeding, to be stitched and bandaged at the doctor's surgery.

Nell valued the concern and companionship of her neighbours. 'Come in,' she said to each of them when they called, but struggled with tears, half-truths, subterfuges, until they were gone.

The postman knocked again. The letter, from the Ministry of Pensions, awarded her 13/9*d* a week for herself and 20/5*d* a week for her children. The total had been calculated at 33/9*d*.

Nell left the letter open on the table. It was still there when George and Andrew rushed in from school.

'What's for tea?' the boys demanded.

'Lay the table,' Nell said.

George picked up the letter and read it. 'This is wrong,' he said. 'They're diddling you out of 5*d* a week.'

Andrew read the letter. 'So they are,' he said.

'Let me see,' Nell said, and checked the figures. 'You're right,' she said. 'I must get that changed.'

From France, Jack had appointed his eldest son George to be Nell's right hand. In the last year of the war, he sent him, on his tenth birthday, a card and a letter.

Just a few lines to wish you many happy returns of your birthday. Dad only wishes he was at home to celebrate it, but he must fight for home and country no matter how much he may long to be with you. Now my dear little son, you must remember you have also got to fight, not out here, but at home looking after and helping your dear mother as much as you can, not only now, but later on, and I know you will do that for you do love your mum and dad with all your heart. The design on your birthday card is a copy of my cap-badge. I had it done by an old French lady in one of the villages behind the lines while out for a few days rest. It is the badge of a regiment that has made a glorious name for itself out here, and I am proud to belong to it. It has been through many battles and has always done well. I hope to be with it when this war finishes, and then you will find that your dad is still the same old loving dad he used to be. I was very pleased to know of those certificates you had earnt so well, for it shows you are a good boy at school as well as at home. Now you must tell your brothers that dad will send them a nice card on their birthdays as well. Give mum a nice kiss and a hug from me and tell her dad do want her so much.

Nell lifted David onto her lap and hugged him. She knew how disappointed he had been not to get a birthday card. All he had to remember his father by were a few memories of his last home leave. She wanted the boy to keep them alive. 'You remember, don't you?' she would say, and remind him of what happened, and hear him talk about it in his child language; of being in bed with his mum and dad, and wriggling out and sitting on top of the bedclothes astride his dad's body; his dad pretending to snore, and his mum getting some tea; pulling his dad's cheeks and hair, and his dad grabbing him and tickling him with loud bursting noises on his neck and ears; laughing himself out of breath; sitting on his dad's knees and being bumped up and down until he was out of breath again; his dad cuddling him and giving him an army prayer book, and thumbing the pages looking for pictures. Sailing up the river in a boat; long, green weeds stretching and wriggling like snakes; dad rowing, and the water bubbling and splashing where the oars dipped and skimmed the surface; feeling safe on mum's lap; his brothers trailing their fingers and grabbing at loose leaves floating near the boat; the bright, green rushes at the edge of the Promenade; the weeping willows, and the dark trees climbing the bank into the clouds; Aunt Lyd steering; Aunt Tilly sitting beside her; the sudden storm; rain throwing hoop-las on the water; mum looking frightened; feeling her body tremble; dad rowing to the bank of the Promenade; everyone getting out except dad and Aunt Tilly who take the boat back; meeting them at the bridge; being wet through; dad giving him a piggy back; dad playing his mouth organ and marching home. Going to the station; dad holding him with one arm; clinging to his neck and grabbing the muzzle of his rifle; cold steel; the khaki uniform rough and tickly; the big, fat kit bag at dad's feet; mum on dad's arm; his brothers standing nearby; a train puffing into the station; steam trapped under the roof of the platform; a smoky smell; dad kissing him and putting him down; dad kissing his brothers; dad giving him and his brothers a penny each; dad holding mum tight and kissing her on the lips; mum whispering and sobbing; dad picking up his kit bag and stepping into the train; dad adjusting the straps on the door and leaning out of the open window; dad saying look after mum; the guard blowing a whistle and waving a green flag; the train puffing out of the station; waving until dad was out of sight, then going home.

Nell, with work to do, could not sit all day thinking about the past, but at night, alone in her room, trying to sleep, she remembered the letter from the Ministry of Pensions. Life comes cheap, she thought. If they had to pay the true value of the killed and wounded, countries could never afford to go to war. She wondered if any of her boys would ever want to be soldiers and fight for their country. Andrew was the most likely. She had seen him playing soldiers with his daddy, and noticed him, smart and disciplined, stand to attention with his arms stiff at the sides and his fingers pointing to the ground. George, too generous and easygoing, would never make a soldier. Pat was too untidy and wayward, and David too dreamy. Sadly nothing mattered. If the country needed them, they would have to go. To a drill sergeant, the most unlikely conscript was a challenge, to be licked into shape. Nell got out of bed, bowed her head and prayed for the peace of the world.

The postman came a third time. When they heard the knock, Andrew and Pat rushed into the passage and had a fight over who should take the official looking letter in the fullscap envelope to their mother. They had a tug-of-war with it and nearly tore it in half. Nell rescued it just in time.

A major general in the War Graves Commission wrote to say that Jack had been registered at Adanac Military Cemetery, Miraumont et Pys.

'I crossed the Channel to marry your father,' Nell said to her boys, 'now I must cross it again to visit his grave.'

The letter launched her back into the past again. When the boys had gone to school, and she was alone in the house, she delved into the box of souvenirs which she kept in the corner cupboard of the front room, and found the silk embroidered postcard, bright with badges, flags, flowers in red, blue, green and gold, which Jack had sent to her from France. She did not need to read the words. She knew them by heart.

'To my dear wife, my darling, my ever loving sweetheart. If all the world were lost to me I'd still rest happy with thy love.'

Now he was lost, at rest in France, lying side by side with his comrades instead of with her. How he loved his regiment, and boasted of its battle honours.

Dettingen 1743 – Guadaloupe – Talavera – Albuhera – Vittoria – Pyrenees – Nivelle – Nive – Orthes – Peninsular – Cabool 1842 – Moodkee – Ferogesha – Aliwal – Sobraon – Sevastopol – Taku Forts – New Zealand – Afghanistan 1878/79 – Suakin – South Africa and the Relief of Ladysmith

In the army, a sergeant, he had some power. When he came out, just after Andrew was born, and worked at the printworks round the corner, he became a nonentity. He loved being the family man, throwing the boys onto his shoulders, playing his mouth organ to them, teaching them football and cricket, but Nell knew he never really settled to civilian life. When war came, she noticed the excitement in his eye. With his old regiment he fought in all their battles from Mons to the Marne and the Aisne; La Bassee, Ypres, Hill 60, the Somme, Arras, Italy, then back to France for the Battle of Albert in which he was killed, 22 August 1918.

Nell reviewed her resources. There was never enough money for a trip to the seaside, let alone France, but she was determined to get there somehow, so she would have to work even harder, save more money, perhaps take a lodger.

'I must let your Aunt Lyd know,' she told George. 'I don't suppose Alf could afford it, with all his family, but Lyd might manage it. We'll go and see them. In the summer holidays.'

Chapter 2

Nell lined up her boys on the same smoky platform at Reading where they had all kissed Jack goodbye. Pat broke ranks, ran up and down and nearly fell over the edge onto the line. George pulled him back.

'Now, stand still,' Nell scolded. 'Here comes the train.'

The high crowned hat, pinned in case of emergencies, and the old tent of a Burberry, impeded Nell as she struggled with the heavy case. George and Andrew, in their best suits, grabbed the handle and helped her into the carriage.

The engine got up steam and puffed out of the station. Pat, in grey hand-me-downs, washed and brushed, fidgeted with the window strap, poked his head out of the window and got a smut in his eye. Nell wiped it with the corner of her sweet scented, embroidered handkerchief.

'Now, be a good boy and sit still,' she said.

Whenever she saw Alf Sedgewick, Nell could not help noticing his resemblance to Jack. He had the same short, stocky build and round, open face capped with tight little curls. He had never gone to war. All his energies had gone into his horses and his marriage. The overcrowded terrace house, noisy and untidy, much too small, accommodated Winnie, his eldest girl, and her husband, bringing up a family of their own in the front bedroom. Flossie, Alf's wife, with a fuzz of dark hair and tearful eyes, worn out, past caring, laughed only at night after drinks at the pub. Alf still worked in the stables at the Isleworth brewery, and wore tough clay cords gathered at the knee, leather braces and belt, an open neck flannel shirt and a creamy silk neckerchief tied at the front.

There was not even standing room, so, as soon as they arrived, Nell's three older boys went out with their cousins and played in the street. David stayed with his mother and sat on her knee.

Nell opened her handbag and showed Alf the letter from the Imperial War Graves Commission.

'Poor old Jack,' said Alf, 'buried in a foreign land.'

Near to tears, he told Nell again how he and Lyd had tried to stop Jack joining the army. He sat in his shirt sleeves, peered into his beer, then raised his arms in exasperation at the memory of it all.

His wife, drinking a glass of stout with Nell, looked watery-eyed as usual, so it was impossible to know if she was crying.

Nell, silent, recovering from tears, waited for Alf to express a wish to visit his brother's grave. It never came. Not wishing to embarrass him, she let it go.

Alf calmed himself with the help of a Woodbine from his waistcoat pocket, turned to David and asked his name. 'Do you like horses?' he asked the boy.

David nodded.

'Would you like to see my 'orses at the stables?'

'Yes, please,' David said.

'You'll enjoy that,' Nell said.

At the brewery, Alf showed young David how he groomed his horses, walking under their bellies. In the evening, home from work, he washed with loud splash noises at the scullery sink. After tea he fed his rabbits, then took his nephew to his allotment.

The boy watched his uncle as he hoed between the cabbages growing in straight rows like green soldiers. When Alf Sedgewick finished his work, the two of them went into the tool shed where they sat side by side on a wooden bench. Alf drank some beer out of a bottle, lit a Woodbine, and showed his strong, brown forearms covered with golden hairs. In high pitched cockney he told stories about himself and Jack when they were children, and the aunt who looked after them and made him give up his rabbits, and made Lyd give up her dog Treacle, and stopped Jack playing his mouth organ. Lyd left her pet with a neighbour, but later found him dead down Lion's Creek, so they washed off the mud and buried him under a hedge where he could listen to the birds.

'That was sad about the dog,' David said. 'Why did you call him Treacle?'

'Golden syrup. That's what he was like. Shiny, sticky and sweet, your

Aunt Lyd used to say.'

Alf Sedgewick slapped a gnat on his cheek, sucked the last of his fag, pinched the butt from his mouth and threw it out of the hut onto the path where it burnt away. Then he filled an old cracked cup with beer and lit another cigarette.

David poked a finger in and out of a hole where a knot had fallen out. He looked down at the basket of vegetables. The earth on the carrots and potatoes was beginning to dry. The carrots were red like the bricks of his house at home. At Isleworth the bricks were grey.

'It's the clay,' his uncle explained, and picked up a bean, curved like a bow, broke it and shared it with the boy. A purple seed fell out and disappeared through a crack in the floor. David wondered if it would grow. He tucked his hands under his thighs where the splintery wood was making them sore. His uncle shared a carrot with him, then took a swig from the bottle and finished his beer. 'Time to go home,' he said, and locked the hut.

Walking side by side on the way back, they talked, and the uncle told his orphan nephew that he must be brave and fight his ways.

'Tell me about the Angel of Mons,' David asked.

'Do you believe in fairies? Peter Pan and all that?'

'I suppose so,' David said.

'Then you 'ave to believe in angels. Some of 'em sleep low down in the fields with the shepherds. At Mons, when all the guns started to fire, they woke up all the angels. The soldiers said they saw one.'

'What did it say to them?'

'It said "Peace. Peace on earth." Then the guns stopped. It all went quiet an' the angels went back to sleep. "Peace on earth." That's what it said. but no one took a blind bit of notice, 'cos no one listens to the angels.'

Lyd Sedgewick, still single, now cook, worked and lived at the big house in St. Margaret's Road. On her afternoon off she went with Nell and the boys to Richmond Park.

The boys rushed upstairs to the open deck of the bus and took front seats. Nell and Lyd sat behind. Strands of brown hair escaped from under Nell's hat and blew in the breeze across her face. She half closed her eyes against the buffeting air, and began to think about the old days. The boys gripped the front rail and made engine noises.

They got off the bus and walked to Richmond Gate and into the park.

The boys raced ahead, but David came back winded to the women and took his mother's hand. The three of them sat down on the dry grass near Kidney Wood. David's brothers romped and shouted far away.

'Remember?' Lyd asked as she unpinned her black straw hat and laid it on the grass.

How could Nell forget? She searched her handbag, took out a photo wrapped in tissue paper as though it was a great treasure, and handed it to Lyd. David jumped up and looked at the picture from over his aunt's shoulder.

The sepia photograph, from a studio which claimed the patronage of HRH the Prince and Princess of Wales, the Duke of Cambridge, and the Prince and Princess of Saxe Weimar, showed Nell seated, wearing a black taffeta full-length skirt and blouse and a double string of pearls. One tiny shoe emerges from the hem of her skirt. Her right hand spreads an open book on her lap. The child's right arm rests on Nell's shoulders. Her other arm leans on a small table with a vase of flowers. Nurse and child are linked in postures of trust and affection. Nell's face has a grape-like roundness and bloom. The white dress of Miss Alice contrasts the heavy, melancholy drapes of the background, the dark panelling of the walls, and the dull exuberance of the aspidistra in its pot on the floor.

From a black box in his gloomy studio, and from a tray of chemicals in a dark room, the photographer contrived a magical epiphany, a showing forth of Nell as a young maiden at the point of womanhood and the creation of her own small world.

'1906,' Lyd said. 'The year of the San Francisco earthquake when all those people were killed.'

Nell, more concerned with her own shattered life, had forgotten the earthquake.

'It's all been rebuilt,' Lyd said. 'Miss Celia was telling me. She went to America a little while back. You would never know there had been an earthquake. It's all back to normal.'

Nell drew what comfort she could from what Lyd told her, and took back the picture. 'My dear little Alice,' she said, and put the photograph safely away. 'I used to call her my little white dove. I often wonder what happened to her.'

'She married a Guards officer. He got back safely after the war. They live in the country. Somewhere near Henley. Miss Celia wasn't so lucky. You know she married that Catholic aristocrat. They divorced. It was a great surprise. That's why she took over the house when her mother died.

She has two little girls at school. She often enquires about you and says what a good nurse you were to Miss Alice.'

'I wonder if the little hussy ever thinks of me,' Nell said. 'I would have liked a little girl. I love my lads. They're good boys, really. Not much trouble. Still, it would have been nice to have a girl to dress up and talk to.'

'Why don't you go and see Miss Celia while you're here?'

'D'you think she'd mind?'

'Mind? Of course she wouldn't mind. She'd love to see you and have a chat about the old days.'

'I can remember as though it was yesterday,' Nell said. 'We came out of the photographer's into the sunshine. Miss Alice was very excited at having her picture taken. She couldn't wait to see how it would turn out. She wasn't a bit interested in the shops, and kept asking how long it would take to get the photo. We got back to the house, and there was Jack, waiting at the gate.'

Nell, seeing Lyd smile, knew then, for sure, that her sister-in-law had arranged it all.

Lyd drew close and took Nell's arm. 'It was love at first sight,' she said.

'I was so serious in those days,' Nell said.

'That's what he liked. He admired your spirit. She'd make a good little soldier, he told me.'

Nell smiled. 'All I did was make him laugh,' she said.

'What an argument that was. All about him being a soldier.'

Nell laid aside her old, worn hat. Strands of dark brown hair hung over her flushed cheeks. She brushed them back and pinned them into place. The soft, brown eyes lit her face. 'Did you know about those Fabian meetings next door?' she asked.

'Sir Humphrey was always going on about them,' said Lyd. 'He hated them. Women meddling in politics. Petticoat Government, he called it.'

'I went to one,' said Nell. 'Miss Celia said I should go. There were writers, politicians, professor people. They said, if the world didn't change it would blow itself to pieces. One woman made my hair stand on end. She said we were feeding an underground monster with guns and ammunition. One day it would break out, vomit up all the armaments, then gorge itself with flesh and blood.'

'She wasn't far wrong,' said Lyd. 'As you know, Alf and I never wanted Jack to join the army. The Jubilee did it. Stirred him up. And that sergeant at the barracks. I told him he was a scoundrel. All he did was laugh. Men. What can you do with them? I'm glad I'm not married.'

The women separated. Lyd, in a dark blue, long sleeved, calf length frock, sat squarely, balanced evenly on her buttocks, her weight supported by both arms behind her, and her legs straight out like a fork under her skirt. 'I was glad when you married,' she said. 'You were everything he wanted.'

Nell, in a light cotton dress, sat on her right thigh, her legs drawn under her, and leaned on the prop of her right arm. With her left hand she picked at dry stalks in the grass and looked thoughtful and sad, her face pale and anxious, her mouth tight and strained. She hardly moved her lips as she spoke of the winter before they married, and Jack's burning letters, and how she would look at the snow and see him in his red tunic, melting the ice and frost.

'What a Christmas that was when he came home and we agreed to marry in the spring, in Jersey where it would be sunny and warm.'

'I never forgave him taking you off so far away among strangers, and not even your own family.'

'I missed you all, but it was a lovely day,' Nell said, abstracted with memories.

David enjoyed hearing her talk. At home, absorbed with work, she had no space or time. Now, looking forward, she asked Lyd to go with her to France, to Jack's grave, then to Jersey, and walk where she and Jack used to go through the woods to Gargate Mill, and to the Common at Normont Point where they had picnics. She took the weight off her right arm and bent forward to balance her body.

'Sounds lovely,' said Lyd without enthusiasm, as though not wishing to make commitments.

With two hands, Nell broke the old, dry bent and threw it away. She picked another golden stem and wound it on her finger for a ring while her thoughts wandered back to her wedding day. She took out another photo, by Laurens of Jersey, of her and Jack soon after they were married. David looked at it with his aunt, then handed it back to his mother, who put it away and snapped the bag tight. At that moment Nell knew she would never come back to see Jack's people again. She felt alone, facing reality. Stretching, bracing herself, she broke free from dreams and called her boys.

They walked along the river to the bridge, and climbed the steps to the busy streets and the bus.

Nell took David to see Miss Celia on the day before the end of the holiday. The other boys wanted to go too, but Nell explained that she could not take them all, so it would have to be David on his own because he was smallest, easiest to manage, and not likely to fidget as much as the others.

Nell had long been reconciled to the fact that Jack, before they met, had once been in love with Miss Celia, his 'Apple Blossom Girl'. Therefore, when Lyd opened the door of the big house in St. Margaret's Road and showed her in to the mistress, Nell felt no embarrassment on that account.

Miss Celia, small and slim, had fair hair, waved in the front and cut short at the back like a boy's. The air smelt sweet as she moved across the room in her lavender dress. 'I am so pleased you have made time on your holiday to come and see me,' she said.

The large front room had patterned carpets and green papered walls hung with pictures. From the ceiling, moulded and patterned like the plaster above the picture rail, hung a chandelier. The handsome sofa and easy chairs were covered with red and white striped chintz. There were many pieces of brightly polished furniture and ornaments, including a crucifix and a little statue of Mary the Virgin in a blue dress. One wall was covered with books.

David perched on his mother's lap and gazed at all these wonders. He had never seen such a room before. Miss Celia told him he was big enough to have a chair of his own. She sat him near the tall front window overlooking the drive, and gave him a big, leather covered book with colour pictures of birds.

Miss Celia told Nell about her two daughters, Connie and Sibyl, and crossed the room to fetch their picture in a silver frame on a small round table near the window. 'Here are my two girls,' she said.

'They're very pretty,' Nell said, and clung to the picture as though not wanting to let it go.

'I'm sorry you won't see them,' Miss Celia said. 'They are with friends at Ropley.'

Nell handed back the photograph. Miss Celia gently kissed the glass before replacing the frame on the table. David looked and saw two smiling girls with their arms round each other.

'How is Miss Alice?' Nell asked.

'Thriving. She has two boys and is expecting again. They live at Hambleden. We had a house there for several years. I often see her. She remembers you with great affection and will be most interested to know we have met.'

'I would like to see her again,' said Nell.

'There is no reason why you should not. Lydia told me where you live. That is not far from Hambleden. I believe there are buses. You must give me your address. When I write to Alice I will ask her to arrange something. Take David with you. He could play with the children. There are always hordes of them about. He would love the garden and the river. Tell me about your other boys, Ellen. You have four, I believe.'

'Oh well, madam, they're just boys. Growing up. Getting into mischief. They worry me sometimes, but I wouldn't be without them. George, my eldest, will soon be starting work.'

'That will help, won't it?' said Miss Celia. 'My dear, we were sorry to hear about Jack. That awful war. So much misery. So many tragedies. Our own family was fortunate, I suppose. Young Dick, Alice's husband, was in the Guards, you know, but got back safe and sound, thank God. My husband was in the diplomatic service. We were in Egypt for most of the war. Our marriage has broken up. That, too, is a kind of tragedy. I am alone, like you, Ellen. I must say, I envy you your boys. I love my girls, of course. We are great friends. Naturally, I would have liked a boy, but it would have to have been as well as, not instead of either Connie or Sibyl. I always say children are like Christmas presents. One waits with great excitement, not knowing what one will get, but when it comes it is treasured. The pleasure of receiving the gift banishes any disappointment at not getting the thing one perhaps hoped for. The baby at one's breast is the baby one loves. Don't you think so, Ellen?'

'When the girls marry you will have your boys, madam.'

'Quite so. And one day you will have your girls. Then there will be grandchildren. My word, we are looking ahead. I do pray for you now, Ellen, and hope the future will make up for all you have suffered and are suffering. I know that it cannot entirely do that. There is nothing which can replace your loss. Let us have some tea.'

Miss Celia pulled the long, red rope near the fireplace. A bell sounded in the distance. A young girl in a black dress, white apron and hat, came with a tray and placed it on the table between the women.

'Please, Mary, pull up a chair for the young gentleman,' said Miss Celia.

It gave David confidence to see his mother at ease in the fairy-tale world of silver tea things and fragile, pink patterned china with gold edging. As they helped themselves, first to buttered toast, then to jam tarts, the ladies talked about the old days. David did not understand it all, but knew that some of it was sad. Miss Celia gave him a napkin for wiping his sticky fingers. She rang the bell again, and Mary came to take the tray away.

'Would you like a different book to read, David?' Miss Celia asked.

'No thank-you,' David said. 'I like birds. The pictures are spiffing.'

The women smiled.

'You will like it at Hambleden, then,' said Miss Celia. 'It is a little late in the year now. The birds have been busy all summer rearing their young. Now they are tired. Some of them have to rest and get their strength back before they fly away to somewhere warm for winter.'

'I know,' David said, 'the warblers and swallows.'

'How clever you are,' Miss Celia said. 'You sound like an expert. You really must go to Hambleden in the spring. Alice and her children will love having you. You will be able to go bird-nesting.'

David returned to his seat near the window. As he turned the pages of the book, he listened to the women talking.

'I remember you used to sing, Ellen. To Alice. Lovely little Scottish lullabies. I used to think how beautiful they were. There was one which particularly appealed to me. *At the back of the North Wind*. The words are George Macdonald's. I looked them up when Lydia told me you were coming.

> Where did you come from, baby dear?
> Out of everywhere into here.

'Fancy you remembering, madam. All those years ago. I'm afraid my singing days are over.'

'I don't believe it,' said Miss Celia. 'It would give me such pleasure to hear you again. There was a sort of carol. *That Holy Thing*. I am sure you must have sung that to David.' She turned to the boy. 'David, you persuade her. I am sure she would do anything for you.'

'Yes, mum. Sing to us,' David said.

Nell's voice, sweet and soft, dropped almost to a whisper as the emotion caught her breath.

> They all were looking for a king
> To slay their foes and lift them high;
> Thou cam'st, a little baby thing,
> That made a woman cry.

Miss Celia clapped eagerly. David joined her. Nell, springing tears, struggled to hold them back. She dived into her handbag for a handkerchief to wipe her eyes. 'Goodness,' she said, 'look at me disgracing myself. Please forgive me, madam.'

'You must make her sing more often, David,' said Miss Celia.

Nell made a move to go.

'Well, we have had a lovely chat,' Miss Celia said. 'I have so enjoyed it. I hope you will come again.'

'Thank-you,' Nell said. 'It's been lovely.'

'Goodbye, David, You will come and see me again, won't you?'

The boy held his mother's hand. Lyd showed them out and said she would be home early so Nell could have a good night out with the family before she went home.

Long after dark, the grown-ups, back from the pub, called the children in from the street and sent them to bed, dirty and unwashed. Nell relaxed her rules and made no fuss. Winnie helped her drunken husband into the front bedroom. In the middle bedroom, Chrissy, the youngest girl, showed herself naked to David and had a fight with Pat and her brother Alfie, the only boy. The four of them shared a bed, both ends, foot and mouth. The beds had no linen; just blankets, and pillows without slips.

Noises, and the snuff of the candle, kept David awake. Winnie played a gramophone and shouted at her husband. Her babies cried. Downstairs, under the noisy gaslight of a smoke-filled room, the adults sat at a table covered with red and green patterned oil cloth smothered with beer bottles and glasses, scraps of bread and butter and cheese, greasy knives and plates. Their gaiety and clamour filled every corner of the house. David felt Pat jump in his sleep and scratch his cheek with his toe nail. He hated the rough, dirty smelling blankets. Fleas were biting.

Suddenly, in the room below, laughter turned to tears. David heard his mother sobbing and decided to go down to her. He got as far as the landing, then saw dimly that two couples sat spooning on the stairs, one pair above the other. Reluctant to disturb them, he went back to bed.

Strange how the tears made the house silent. Winnie stopped the gramophone, soothed her children and spoke softly to her husband. The lovers moved from the stairs to go out of doors for their last embraces. The older girls came tip-toeing on a scented path to the back bedroom. The sobbing ceased. The other grown-ups climbed into their creaking beds in the two rooms downstairs.

David, falling asleep at last, dreamed of a hawk. The eyes of a dove burned in the clutch of its talons. The boy's gun, too heavy to lift, turned into a peashooter. The face of his mother faded.

In the morning, Nell and her boys went home.

Chapter 3

Home was at Reading, Cheese Row, number 26, in a fret of terraces. The houses, all alike, knitted together like the wool of a garment, plain stitch, were built on land, once flat meadow just above the flooded margins of the River Thames. Nell's house, in the middle of a terrace, faced the sun. She lived cheek-by-jowl with her neighbours in a sort of slaves row, each household free within the limits of the family income. No one had cash at the bank. Any money in hand was waiting to be paid away.

At the school in Cheese Row, at Christmas, David learnt to sing carols about a Virgin's womb. 'What is a womb?' he asked his mother.

'A place of safety where a baby lives in a mother's body until it is born,' Nell said, 'like a bird's egg.'

David's geography mistress said the town was a confluence. She drew a triangle on the blackboard and marked the sides. 'Thames', 'Kennet' and 'Chilterns'. In the middle of the triangle she drew what looked like a bird's egg and marked it 'Reading'.

The history teacher took David's class to see the Abbey ruins. The old stone walls were covered with ivy. On one of the walls there was a tablet with some music written by a monk. The lively song, with its strange words, made the boy think of sunshine and holidays and bird-nesting.

> Summer is icumen in,
> Lhude sing cuccu!
> Groweth sed, and bloweth med,
> And spring'th the wude nu –
> Sing cuccu!

24

The history teacher said Reading was a fortress; battleground for Iron Agers, Romans, Saxons, Danes, Normans, Plantagenets, Tudors, Stuarts and Orangemen. Once there had been a castle, built by one king and destroyed by another.

Nell had kept the issue of *The Jersey Evening Post* with which she and Jack had entertained themselves on their wedding day. She had folded the yellowing pages and used them as a lining for her box of mementoes. Now she took everything out, unfolded the newspaper, and read again the report from America concerning a Mrs. Decker who told President Roosevelt that a woman was as good as a man at making a home and providing for her children.

That was what she must do. She would make the house a place of safety and a fortress for her sons. Nothing would harm them. They would grow into men of whom their father would be proud. And she would go to Adanac War Cemetery, kneel at his grave and whisper to him that all was well.

She often told George that she could not keep up sides with it. Money coming in was not enough for rent, coal, gas, food and clothes. That was why, to make ends meet, she scrubbed floors and took in people's washing. Monday was always a steaming, sud-smelling, miserable day. Somehow, she kept her head above water, but, to save money to go to France, she had to take a lodger.

She really wanted a young woman, but, when Jim Wilmot came to her door and said he had known Jack in some barracks before the war, and was desperate for somewhere to live, she took pity on him, let him inside, and he stayed. In the beginning she had notions he might be a father-figure. Instead, he added to her burdens.

Wilmot, without a job, paid Nell out of his dole and army pension. Also, he bought pigs trotters from the abbattoirs, scalded and shaved them, and sold them to his cronies. In the back garden he built a chicken-run and kept fowl. On the boundary wall he grew loganberries, big and juicy, fed with chicken manure, and with dung from the abbattoirs.

The lodger, a big man, wore old army clothes, kept them cleaned and pressed, polished his boots, washed and shaved every day, brushed his hair and retained a certain self-respect. Somehow, he paid his way, and, out of a meagre surplus, backed horses, boozed, and, when drunk, taunted and threatened. 'You oughta gerout a bit more, mishish. 'Ave a bit o' fun. Yer 'ubby wouldn't mind. Them Surreys was a randy blurry lot. Terrible reputation. Alwaysh after the women.'

Nell responded with a tight-lipped, silent reproach. In the war, Wilmot had been a horse and mule man on the home front. The neighbours despised him as a drunken parasite. Molly, a fat old wire terrier, his only friend and retinue, followed him everywhere. The old bitch, though affectionate to the family, could be fierce with strangers, and was sometimes muzzled.

Nell came to regard Wilmot as the enemy within, but, as long as he paid his way, she fed him and his dog. She blamed herself for letting him in, but found excuses for him, and, weary from work, she had not the will and energy to throw him out.

Saturdays, Nell shopped and took David with her. On the way home they called on Gran, Nell's mother, the boy's only grandparent. Gran lived with her unmarried daughter in the front downstairs room of her youngest son's house in Rotten Row. The garden backed onto Nell's in Cheese Row. A hole in the fence made the two backyards a common playground.

Inside the house, there wasn't an inch to spare. The walls bulged with David's cousins. Gran's small room, choc-a-bloc and stuffy, was full of furniture and utensils. There was no room to move, so Gran seldom got up from her armchair. Her pale, puffed hands rested on her enormous belly. David thought she looked like the solemn, plump Queen whose picture decorated a Diamond Jubilee mug on the mantelpiece.

Nell had brought her mother a bag of groceries and was stowing the items away in corners and cupboards. 'Come round some time,' she said to Gran. 'Come and have a chat.'

Gran hated Wilmot. 'Not while he's there,' she said. 'Why don't you get your brothers to throw him out?'

'I will. Some time,' Nell said.

'It's a scandal,' Gran said.

Her three brothers wanted to throw him out, but Nell kept putting them off, so they lifted their hands in despair, excused themselves, and seldom visited their sister because of her lodger. Occasionally they came with a little silver for the boys, but, like the neighbours, without understanding. Probably they suspected some hanky-panky. Nell, a Jesus woman, had, from the highest motives, crossed the road for Wilmot, but, if that old Priapus had tried anything on, she, like Hesta of the Hearth, would have driven the old goat away with a crumpled horn.

Nothing shook Nell's resolve to sacrifice herself. She had no respite because, for the boys, there was no closed season for dirty, dangerous pursuits. After autumn scrumping came Guy Fawkes night. Fireworks gone, the bonfire smouldering into darkness, boys rampaged across fences, flower beds and vegetables, and disturbed the hen-houses. By Christmas, Nell had forgotten their mischief and filled their stockings with fruit and chocolate. She added a box of paints, or a piece of Meccano or a book. George had *Hereward the Wake*, Andrew *The Three Musketeers*, Pat *Robinson Crusoe* and David *Greek Heroes*. Each had a Bible. From the depths of her faith she wrote in a copybook hand, 'The blessing of the Lord it maketh rich, and he addeth no sorrow with it.'

At Christmas, the British Legion gave war orphans a party at the Comrades Club. There was always a magician. He showed the roaring children an empty topper, black as pitch, and put a silver cloth over it and told a few jokes. Then he waved a wand and produced little white doves from the empty hat. David told his mother he would like to have brought one home for her.

The boys made no New Year resolutions, but slid into winter on frozen pavements and ice covered meadows. To fight cold they made winter warmers of smouldering rags in cocoa tins with holes to blow through for keeping the rag aflame. They stuffed these tins in their jackets. Nell forbade it, but they did it just the same, and their coats came burnt and stinking to the wash.

The thaw flooded fields in the backs between the Thames and the terraces. On rafts of discarded fencing they pirated the waters on voyages of discovery. Pat sailed further, stayed longer afloat and got wetter than the rest.

As days lengthened, the boys sought adventure in woods and meadows, and shared the banks of the river with riparian owners, and kingfishers whose nest holes, deep in the mud, smelled of corruption from meals of water nymphs and minnows. Along the two rivers and their margins, they jumped about timber barges, rolled down grassy slopes, scrabbled in chalk pits, and tore their clothes climbing trees and fences. To get somewhere quick they hung on the tail-boards of carts and lorries, or raced on penny an hour bone-shaker bikes without brakes. They wore out their boots pushing on single skates, and kicking stones, tins, bottles, sorbos, string and paper balls and anything else lying in their paths. On pavements and in gutters they played fag cards and marbles. They ran with the steamers.

KEEP OUT the notice said, but it meant nothing to the boys of Cheese Row, intent on an early Sunday morning swim. From all along the street they gathered in the Warren across the bridge, clambered over the fence, and rushed under the trees to the pitcher on the river bank. From the diving board David peered into the magic of the water where the summer sun searched the shallows. When the others jumped in, splashed, the magic disappeared. It did not belong to him anyway, so the law came and took it away.

'Not another Sedgewick,' the policeman said to David, having already taken the names of George, Andrew and Pat. 'Are there any more of you?'

'No, sir,' said David, curly like his father, and with his mother's soft, brown eyes. 'I'm the last.'

'I'll be along to see your dad,' said the officer.

'We haven't got a dad,' George said. 'He was killed in the war.'

The policeman closed his little black book. 'Don't let me catch any of you down here again,' he said.

David told his mother that there was a row of medal ribbons on the bobby's navy blue tunic. 'Like a rainbow,' he said.

'Well, then, perhaps everything will be alright,' Nell said, because she believed in such signs.

Where did she find the strength to sustain such hope? The pastor had offered a banqueting house, but when she called on him she came away empty. She had been to his church, but found it high with incense and, more in need of warmth than smoke, had not returned.

The Scottish Presbyterian Church opposite the school in Cheese Row was always open. After lessons, children burst in to try and solve the puzzle of the church with this strange name. David discovered his mother kneeling there. After her work she had come to say the Lord's Prayer. She beckoned David to come and sit beside her. His companions left them to themselves. Nell finished her prayer, took the boy's hand and walked home.

George and Andrew had paper rounds and took Pat to learn the ropes. Weekends they washed crockery at a coffee stall. In summer they ran with the river boats, performed tricks, and the trippers threw them coins. David, the only drone, ran errands for everybody and got tips for delivering trotters and clean laundry. The money did not all go into the family exchequer. Each of the boys had a saving tin, and, with a knife blade, slid out coins for marbles and alleys, sorbos, fireworks, steel hoops and hooks, second-hand skates, and for the hire of broken down bikes for a penny an hour.

The family sought any cheap or free supply of food. Factory girls in the street sold their weekly allowances of broken biscuits. From the greengrocer they bought 'specs' – fruit on the turn. Nell made a fruit-cake every Sunday. By Monday morning it had all been eaten, so David was sent to the cakeshop for stale left-overs at cut prices.

The household was having tea.

'Big ripe Victorias the size of cricket balls,' said Wilmot. 'And them dustmen knockin' 'em down with their brooms.'

He slumped heavily in the armchair, a Windsor near the coal cupboard. Once, it had been Jack's chair in which he leaned back with his head on the wall and played his mouth organ. The grease patch on the faded wallpaper had become a sacred spot, never cleaned off. The chair had been Jack's throne, his seat of power, a wool-sack for law and order. Now he was gone, Nell ruled from an old stool the other side of the hearth. She had allotted the armchair to Wilmot to help him in the role she hoped he would play, but, too often, he used it as a flop seat to slump into with a belly of beer, and study form.

'Where were these plums?' George asked.

'In one 'o the 'ouses over the bridge, the other side of the church,' said Wilmot.

'That's on our paper round,' said Andrew. 'We'll get some tomorrow.'

'You be careful,' Nell warned. 'That's stealing. You could be prosecuted.'

'Don't be daft, woman,' Wilmot said. 'They'll be alright. No one's goin' to see them that time o' the mornin.'

But it was the act itself, as much as the consequences, which worried Nell. She sat opposite Wilmot on the other side of the open range. There was always a fire, except on the hottest days of summer, and the big, black kettle always on the hob. Behind her, one step down, she had everything to hand – the scullery with its gas oven, earthenware sink, bread pan, copper and mangle, food and crockery shelves, dish cloths and towels. Nell and Wilmot, like adversaries, faced different ways, government and opposition. He started trouble. She put it right.

'There's nothing wrong with scrumping, picking up windfalls,' she said. 'but knocking down fruit off trees is stealing. Don't do it.'

Grim faced, she organised them, cuffed their misdeeds. She allowed
their fun and games, but set limits. The boys, young and self-willed, took
her for granted as provider, respected her as prefect, and looked out for
her rare smile, welcome as winter sun. She made no speeches outside the
home, rarely said anything memorable, and made few demands, even of
Wilmot who, after drunkenness, said he was sorry, emptied his pot and
cleaned up his mess.

In the early morning the three older boys talked as they dressed to go
to their paper rounds.

We'll get some of those plums,' Andrew said.

'D'you think we should?' George queried. 'P'raps mum's right.'

'Why should them dustmen have them all? If they can take them so
can we.'

'What about if we're caught?' George asked.

'I'll keep scib,' Pat said. He would watch for policemen.

'You keep out of it,' George said, knowing Pat's bent for getting into
trouble.

When George and Andrew came home for breakfast without their
younger brother, Nell became anxious. She fretted over Pat. When one
of his hens hatched her chicks, Wilmot put them into a small wire cage all
to themselves. Always, one chick got away. Pat was like that. Nell could
not keep him under her wing. He would not come to her call.

'Where've you been?' Nell challenged Pat when he came home. She
dragged the story out of him, bit by bit. Haunted by a policeman on a
bicycle, George and Andrew decided against plundering the fruit. Pat
felt cheated. When he saw the constable disappear over the horizon, he
ran off to find Tom Stevens from next door, and Ted Childs from down
the road. He told them about the plums and they went with him to knock
some down. The policeman backtracked and caught them at it. He took
names and addresses and told them they would be summoned.

'You little rascal,' Nell exploded, and stiffened her trembling lips and
looked fierce. In these fits of rage she hit out. They did not last long.
Afterwards, in quieter mood, she bowed her head in shame. Against her
nature, she thorned and spiked and prickled herself into curbing her
wild, arse-of-the-trouser-tearing, stone-kicking, tree-climbing, cave-
burrowing, food-snatching boy children, the four of them.

Mrs. Stevens came round to talk to Nell about these events over the
dregs of breakfast tea. 'Silly little buggers' she said.

Nell found excuses. 'It was Jim Wilmot. He edged them on' she said.

'Let 'im pay the bloody fines, then. The old devil, gettin' them into trouble. I don't know 'ow you puts up with 'im.'

Nell's neighbours sympathised, admired her fight, her diligence, but saw her through a glass darkly, without understanding, and were ill at ease and out of tune with the long-suffering, conscientious quality of her life. Without being a gossip, Nell, through her children, kept on good terms with her neighbours. Because of the span of their ages, the boys had friends in all the echelons. Each age group had its own football, bird-nesting, steamer-running, river-swimming, paper-round teams. David was seldom in any joint undertaking with his elder brothers. By the time he caught up with one scene, they had gone on to other, more adult pursuits.

On the day of the summons David, on his way home from school, saw Wilmot staggering drunkenly. It was rent day. The landlord, Mr. Goodenough, plump and red faced, stood at his mother's door. Neighbours, holding rent books, looked on and gossiped. Mrs. Titcombe cast a censorious eye. Mrs. Cotterell leaned with plump arms on her gate and laughed noisily. Mrs. Stevens glared at Wilmot. 'You drunken old sod,' she shouted. 'You're a disgrace to the neighbourhood.' Mrs. Beaseley, behind a half open door, stood dumb and neutral, not wishing to get involved. Her family kept themselves apart. Her little girl was always too clean and well dressed for street games. The father, a butt, picked up dead matches and bits of wood from the gutter, put them in a canvas bag and took them home for the fire. With the money he saved he bought his son a new bike. The machine, polished and shining, was kept out of the public gaze and used only on rare occasions, like a royal coach.

Wilmot shouted aggressively, 'Go insi' de lot o' you. Min' yer own damn bishnesh.' He waved the women indoors, but they stayed and stared.

The landlord had bought the houses as security for his old age. He kept a bakers' shop. His daughter taught David at Sunday school. The boy worshipped her as a sort of goddess, tall, fair and beautiful. She responded with favours, held his hand and sent him happily away with texts for his mother. Sunday school over, the children stampeded into a narrow alley blind to the main road where trams went grinding up and down hill to-and-from Caversham and the town. David, at the front of the herd in the alley, pushed into the track of a tram, might have ended up as pressed veal. The driver let down the cow-catcher, but the tram pushed David along on its bumper until it stopped. Passengers got out and stared. Passers-by stopped and crowded round. The landlord's daughter pushed through the crowd, comforted him and led him home, as any goddess should.

Wilmot wobbled and shouted beligerently to the landlord. 'Ulloh yer ol' money grabber. Come for yer pound o' flesh ol' mate?'

Nell pushed him through the doorway, 'Get inside and go to bed, you silly old fool,' she scolded.

'Shorry, mishish,' Wilmot said, and lurched round to make a final gesture of defiance at the neighbours. 'Goo nigh' ladish. 'Appy dreams,' he bawled, and waved them all goodbye. He lumbered along the passage past David, then struggled upstairs to bed.

The women assembled at Nell's gate. They attempted to console her, then went home and shut their doors.

Inside, Nell sat on her stool and gazed into the fire. 'They're all very kind,' she said, but looked comfortless.

David perched on her knee.

Nell, with her back to the light of the window, gripped the rent book with her right hand. Her other arm rested on the scrubbed table. She gazed at the lines of a shove ha'penny board scored by Jack before the war. Wherever she looked, reminders of him haunted her. She hugged David for comfort and told him how she would have liked a little girl. She meant no harm, but the boy felt the guilt of being her last chance. He had disappointed her. He wished he had been Miss Alice, and seen his mother as she and his father had seen her, when she was young and beautiful and happy. A strange, impossible desire born of envy of the two people to whom his mother had been most devoted.

'Lay the table and we'll have some tea,' she said. 'I wonder where young Pat has got to.'

Pat came in while David was setting the table. Nell had cleaned and tidied him for the police court in the morning, but now, after dags and dares with his mates on the way home from school, he looked dirty and unkempt.

'Go and wash,' Nell told him. 'And don't forget, my lad, no pocket money until that fine is paid. P'raps that will teach you a lesson.'

Pat could not complain. Tom Stevens had been punished the same way. Ted Childs had been given a leathering as well. His father worked in the brewery, came home drunk and belted his wife and children. When

Mrs. Childs died suddenly, the eldest girl, her father's favourite, who escaped the beatings, looked after the family. Going out in the evenings, she rouged, powdered and perfumed herself, and dressed up as a flapper in short skirts and high heels. Street kids mocked and bawled at this sex symbol of Cheese Row. All she did was laugh.

Pat grinned at David, poked him in the ribs, and rushed into the scullery to wash at the sink.

Chapter 4

What was the mystery behind Nell's trembling hand? Some blast, stirring strings and sinews, drove her into a compulsion of activity, backwards and forwards, arms and legs in perpetual motion. David, ill with flu, lying beside her, sleepless at night, felt her shaking like a leaf in the wind. It was she who needed the nursing, and, when he was better, the doctor turned his attention to Nell and bullied her to bed.

Gran would not come, nor any of the relations, so Nell went to see her friend Tilly Hurst who lived in the country the other side of the river in the Chilterns. The two women had become friends in the war when they worked together at a riverside hotel and shared left-overs of dripping, suet and lard.

Nell did not have to ask for help. All she did was explain the situation. Tilly said 'Say no more, gal. I'll come.'

Tilly left her two children with an aunt who lived near, went to look after Nell for a week, and slept in her bed. Tall and big framed, she stood no nonsense from Wilmot, who kept out of her way and behaved himself. She had a classic beauty, with a bush of red hair which she tamed somehow with pins and combs, but always some wisps of it gossamered her face and glinted gold in the sun. One could imagine a god coming down to her in a shower of gold.

It was August Bank Holiday, but David was more housebound than ever, running errands and doing odd jobs for Aunt Tilly. Ambitious, beginning to kick the traces, needing money to spend, he showed his restlessness. When he tripped on the back doormat and cut his head on the bread pan, Tilly bandaged him and called him a wounded soldier.

'What's the matter?' Tilly asked.

'I want to go out,' David said.

'Why don't you go then?'

'I want to run the steamers,' said David, who felt the urge to prove himself to his swaggering, overbearing brothers.

'Run with the steamers, then,' said Tilly, as though it was the easiest thing in the world.

'They won't let me,' David explained. Illness had enhanced his reputation as a weakling, a mother's boy, hugged on her knee and in her bed. 'George says I'm too young.'

'Well, perhaps you are,' said Tilly. 'You won't know until you try.'

'I can do all the tricks.'

'I bet you can.'

'Not like Fatty. He's a runner, but he falls in a heap when he tries to do a handstand.'

'He's a friend of Andrew's, isn't he?'

'He's in Andrew's gang. The Dauntless Five. They all call me a milksop.'

'That's because you've been ill. You're better now. Pat runs with the steamers, doesn't he?'

'He runs with *River Queen*. That's a small boat. He says he'll punch my nose if I barge in on his lot.'

Pat suspected favouritism, but, in the share out of food, clothes, cuffs for misdeeds, his younger brother was no favoured sibling. It was just that David was more in tune with his mother. In winter, on the coldest days, Nell drew his arm under her red knitted shawl and, like a secret, held his arm snugly against her body. Pat noticed this closeness and harboured grievances against his brother.

'What about George and Andrew?' asked Aunt Tilly. 'What boats do they run with?'

'George runs with *Britannia*. That's the one I like. She's lovely. All white with green edges. Andrew runs with *The Empress of India*. She's brown. She's the biggest.'

Some were big and some were small. Some went upstream, some went down. Gangs of boys fought for the right to run with certain steamers. Spheres of influence were jealously guarded. David understood the difficulty. An extra runner meant less share of the money all round.

'Why don't you go and try your luck?' said Tilly.

'What will mum say?'

'Don't worry. You leave mum to me. Off you go.'

David's Aunt Tilly boosted morale with her bright assurance that he was equal to his brothers. She waved him away. In the passage, at the foot of the stairs, he shouted goodbye to his mother.

Tilly took Nell a cup of tea.

'Where's young David?' Nell asked.

'Gone to run with the steamers,' Tilly said.

'That's naughty. He should be helping you.'

'Don't worry, gal. I told him to go.' Tilly sat on Nell's bed. 'He's a bright lad,' she said.

'I'm afraid sometimes,' Nell said. 'There's so much danger down that river. I know I can't hold him back, but I do worry.'

'George will look after him, won't he?'

'He'll do what he can,' Nell said, but she knew that George would have to deal with the discrimination of older boys. In their world, harrassed into self-reliance by parents, police and private owners, it was every man for himself. David would be considered a burden and an embarrassment.

'It must be rotten being the youngest,' Tilly said.

'They bully him a bit,' Nell said.

'That's good,' said Tilly. 'It'll make him fight. He'll survive, like the rest of us.'

Nell knew that David would not be allowed to run with the steamers, but she enjoyed Tilly's cockney perkiness. Her friend lived in the country, but she was a Londoner, and had the Londoner's self-confidence and optimism.

'You always make me feel better,' Nell said.

'That's the ticket,' Tilly said. 'Drink your tea, gal, and have a little sleep. Forget your troubles.'

The steamers, moored each side of the old iron bridge, were being washed, polished, provisioned for their afternoon trips. David jumped on *Britannia*'s landing stage, lay on his stomach and, through the open boards, searched the shallows for small gudgeon skirmishing in the sun on the sandy bottom of the river.

'Blimey if it isn't the nipper,' George said.

David turned on his elbows and looked up at his brother.

'I want to run with the steamers,' he said.

'You're too little. You're not old enough. What's up with your head?' David told him. 'It doesn't hurt,' he said. 'I can do all the tricks. Anything you tell me.'

'Slip 'im one across the ear and send 'im 'ome,' said Fatty.

David showed his brother how he could do cartwheels and walk on his hands. Then he offered to swim a width of the river, and stand on his head on the parapet of the old iron bridge. The runners, with a long wait before the steamers sailed, welcomed the diversion. 'Let's see what he can do,' they said, and watched him perform his feats.

'Want to have a go at it, Fatty?' Andrew asked his mate, and all the runners laughed.

'We'll soon have you running the steamers,' George said.

'I want to run today,' David said.

'Not today,' George said. 'You go home and help Aunt Tilly.'

David's pride would not allow him to return home too soon, so he found some boys his own age and played wounded soldier in the old army tank which stood on a concrete platform at the end of the Promenade near the bridge.

Tilly had to go at the end of the week. Gran said 'I'll come if that old devil Wilmot keeps out of the way.'

On a rain slanting, wet window-pane morning, Gran, working in the scullery, scowled at Wilmot's cut-throats on the window-sill above the sink. There were two, one for shaving himself, the other for shaving trotters. Gran carried the dripping clothes from the sink to the mangle. David stood and watched. The old iron machine, with its splintery wooden rollers, capable of crushing fingers and hands, was full of threat.

'Don't get in my way,' Gran scolded, and stirred the clothes still boiling in the copper.

The boy ran upstairs to his mother, lying back on her pillows. Her long, brown hair, unpinned, fell about her shoulders. Her hands, horny with work, trembled on the white overlap of the sheet. The medicines on the bedside table gave the room an unusual, unfeminine smell.

'Fetch my box, David,' she said.

He went downstairs and into the front room, his mother's pride and joy. At God knows what expense of nerve and tissue she had gathered it together. Everything shone; the maroon coloured rexine of sofa and chairs; the red patterned lino; the dark mahogany of the upright piano and china cabinet; the black leaded grate; even the leaves of the aspidistra on the table under the window. He opened the corner cupboard, took out the light mahogany box and carried it upstairs.

David watched as his mother took out the souvenirs one by one. The bent bullets, the blood stained German forage cap she handled impatiently and set on one side. The French blue bead necklaces, the brooches and crosses she fingered lovingly. There were wads of old letters and postcards. She untied the tapes and started to read. 'I must read these alone,' she thought. 'I cannot trust myself in front of him.'

'Why don't you go and help your Gran,' Nell said.

'There's nothing to do,' David said.

'Put out the aspidistra,' Nell said. 'It needs a good soaking. You could manage that, couldn't you?'

Back in the front room, David took out *Greek Heroes* from the cupboard and browsed through the colour pictures of Perseus, Heracles, Orion, Achilles, Odysseus and Jason. Then he looked at one of his mother's books, *The Allegory of the Cross*. The pictures showed a boy, dressed in a sort of nightshirt, in dire situations; lost in a blizzard, storm tossed at sea, desolate on a hillside, threatened by wild animals. In these valley of the shadow of death adventures the boy, a type of John Bunyan child Christian, hugged a golden cross which no one could take from him, not even armed bandits. The illustrations made a deep impression. To drive away sadness he played the phonograph. There were only two cylinders, *Home Sweet Home* and *The Old Rustic Bridge*.

Gran came waddling in. 'Stop that noise,' she grumbled.

David braked the machine and took off the cylinder. 'I'll put out the aspidistra,' he said.

'Be careful you don't drop it, then,' said Gran.

Every spring Nell showed David the new shoots pushing up at the base of the plant. The boy could not match her enthusiasm. He wanted a geranium. In Cheese Row, only the poorest families had an aspidistra, or nothing, in the front window. A geranium was a badge of prosperity. Careless of the plant, and of Gran's warning, he tripped at the front door. The pot cracked open on the brick path, and the plant spewed into a heap near the gate.

Gran came angrily, cuffed her grandson and pulled him aside. 'You clumsy boy,' she shouted. 'Now, you just go upstairs and tell your mother what you've done.'

Nell put down the letter she was reading. 'Now what's the matter,' she asked David.

He stared at the floor and told her.

Nell offered her hand. 'It's my fault,' she said. 'I shouldn't have asked you. It was too heavy.'

The windows streamed; cried from pain and sorrow, the hopelessness and loss. David went downstairs. Nell listened for noises to tell her what was happening. The rain stopped and the sun burst through. Gran shouted to David to clean up the mess. The front door banged. David, with a broom nearly twice his size, cleaned up the debris of the aspidistra. Nell pictured him struggling, and smiled to herself. She waited for him to come back in and bang the door. It did not happen.

Gran came up. 'He's gone,' she said. 'Slung his hook, the little devil.'

Britannia looked a queen. Geraniums crowded her rails. Flags, bunting, streamers, fluttered her canopies. Sunlight bounced off the water and flickered restlessly on her shining white bows. David saw George, and expected to be sent away. Instead, his brothers treated him to lard cake at the coffee stall.

Young tearaways in straws, striped jackets and flannels, jollied their girls and filed up the gangway. Older men in bowlers and navy blue serge followed their wives on board. A woman played a twangy piano. A young man strummed a banjo. Men drank beer from the bottle. Everyone sang *I'm forever blowing bubbles*. Trippers leaned over the rails of *Britannia* and watched the runners limber up with cartwheels and handstands.

Noah at the flood, the Argonauts and Ulysses faced the dangers of deep waters. Great explorers have risked death from pirates, man-eating cannibals, reefs, rocks, icebergs, storm and tempest. Without some entertainment, a little drunkenness at the outset, to take their minds off the hazards of their enterprises, they might never have left port. The runners were part of the ancient tradition of jollity at the spread of sail. George looked tolerantly at David's debut.

The captain shouted orders. Ropes were untied. *Britannia* steamed free, westward with the sun. On the narrow, broken tow path beyond the Promenade, David stumbled, felt pain, feared he might fail. George rallied him from behind. 'Stick it, kid. That stitch won't last long.' Coins were thrown. The blue walled railway embankment was converging with the river. 'Throw a penny and knock a brick out of the wall, gents,' the runners shouted to the trippers hanging on the rails.

The lock was bright with flowers. Elms and willows cast their shade. The keeper pushed on the long baulk arm of the gate and checked the runners with cautionary glances. Trippers scrambled sweets and coins, handed down cake and lemonade. George cut David down to size and pruned him of any notions of equality and fraternity. 'Better not go any further, kid,' he said. 'Hang around here until we get back.'

In the meadows, David, exhausted, stretched on the grass. Rainbows sparkled in the sweat of his half closed eyes. He jingled the money in his pockets, fingered the milled edges of the coins and counted his riches. His mind blazed with red geraniums. He had seen them on *Britannia*, and in the lock, and in the gardens on the other side of the river. How bright and brave they looked with their red badge flowers and their shield-like leaves. His brain took a sudden leap. He would buy his mother a geranium to replace the aspidistra.

He waited for *Britannia* as for a sweetheart. She came like Victory, flaunting flags streaming in the breeze. In the hard run back, coins dragged, jingled, chafed his thighs and fell out of his cartwheels. He paddled for pennies which dropped short and sank in the water, searched in the mud, lagged behind, and struggled to catch up.

At journey's end, trippers chose him for special reward. Women pointed him out to their men. 'That's the one. Give it to him. Poor little mite.' Interlopers joined the scramble for spoils. Pat, who had run upstream with *River Queen* jostled for extra cash from *Britannia*. David crawled away from the mauls, his hands and feet bruised and bleeding.

On his way home he thought again about what he should do with the money. His wants were endless. Feelings of guilt assailed him. Gran would box his ears. His mother had cried over the loss of the aspidistra. It seemed a waste of tears. A geranium would be different. He tried to imagine his mother's pleasure at receiving one. He felt too tired. The shops were shut. It would have to wait. He dragged himself along.

Nell heard the door, the dash along the passage and the rush upstairs. She heard Gran shouting for David's blood. When he came in she turned and spoke. 'Ah. It's you, David. Where've you been all day? You look as though you've been drawn through a hedge backwards.'

'I've been running the steamers,' David said. 'I got some money. Look.'

He emptied his pockets and piled the money on his mother's bed for an offertory.

Gran shouted from below.

Nell answered with uneasy effort. 'It's alright, mother. Don't bother coming up.'

David, in all his dirt, clambered on the bed and felt the cool, white sheets against his face. He held his mother's rough cut hand and felt it tremble.

'I want to buy you a geranium,' he said.

'That will be lovely,' Nell said, and looked down at him with shining eyes. He had repaid her a thousandfold.

Tomorrow, Sunday, all the shops would be shut. On Monday it was back to school. Beyond that, David could not think. Probably, he would never buy the geranium, but, for Nell, the intention was enough. He fell asleep in her quivering arms.

Chapter 5

While Nell was abed she did some thinking. She decided there would
never be a Fabian Utopia. Politics were just a bit of fun for children. At
general elections, when the school became a polling booth, her boys,
with the patriotism of their father, roamed the streets streaming blue
ribbon for the Tories against red Liberals and black and yellow
Socialists. They scattered leaflets, put them under door knockers and
through letter-boxes, and sang

> Vote, vote, vote for Major Cadogan.
> Chuck old Hastings in the sea...

Nell stood aside and let them enjoy themselves, but no election poster
ever appeared in her window.

In their classrooms they were shown the red on the map, then taken to
the British Empire Exhibition at Wembley where they saw the North
American rodeo and came back wild as cowboys. At school they were
caned, boxed on the ears, smitten with pointers and no questions asked.
At home they needed a firmer hand.

When she was about again, Nell persuaded them to join set-ups of
good order and disipline. the three older boys joined the Church Lads
Brigade and marched with drums and bugles to the mockery of

> We are the Boys Brigade
> All covered in marmalade.
> A tuppeny ha'penny pill box
> And a kettle drum on parade.

David joined the Band of Hope. It was run by the man who kept the Coffee Stall which encouraged labourers to drink tea or coffee instead of beer on their way home from work. George, Andrew and Pat, in turn, had all earned money there helping with the washing up. Then it was David's turn. The stall holder, short and stocky, wore steel rimmed spectacles and had a wiry, black beard. Teetotal, a pillar of the Free Church, he persuaded David to sign the pledge.

For washing and drying the crocks the boy got a few pence and a lard cake at closing time. At the end of the day the two of them went outside to put up the shutters. They ducked under a low trap-door to get back inside where they were alone, cut off from the world. When the man gave David his cake he cuddled him and rubbed the boy's face with his beard. When he gave David the money he put his hand inside the lad's trouser pocket and had a good feel round his privates. David, though surprised, took no offence. He guessed that the man did it to his own children, and had done it to the three brothers before him. He suffered no hurt. The man's hands were plump and red and cold. He probably had a warm heart.

At the Band of Hope David learned preachy, evangelical stanzas and became a real bigot about strong drink. Jim Wilmot told him not to be so daft. On doctor's orders, Nell was drinking Wincarnis for her nerves. David saw her drinking the wine and gave her a long spiel about the evils of intoxicating liquor. His mother erupted with rage. It was a wonder she did not knock his head off. Instead, she got the black lead brushes and did not speak to David again until she had worked out her anger on the shine of the kitchen range. Afterwards she cuddled him and made it up.

In the autumn, under the Salvation Army banner of 'Blood and Fire', Nell made her pilgrimage to Adanac War Cemetery, Miraumont et Pys. Someone took a picture of her kneeling at Jack's grave. It shows her slight figure, head bowed, face darkened by the wide brim of a high crowned hat stuck with pins. She holds a wreath on the stone cross. It must have been a wet, miserable day. She is wearing an old Burberry buttoned to the neck. In the silence she heard the sighs of the dead heroes in the Asphodel Fields, and Jack telling her that he wished to live in the blood of his children. They were the only hope for the future.

Nell came back from France with a new resolve. She joined the Salvation Army because of the help it had given her to visit Jack's grave. Then she persuaded her boys to do the same. War had been her undoing, but the Army in which the family was now conscripted, far from leading men to their death, was one in which wives and husbands, sons and daughters fought side by side to save mankind from its folly. Enlisted for battle, her sons, Jack's sons, put on peak caps and red jersies with flaming stars, and became soldiers for Jesus under a banner of 'Blood and Fire'. They went straight into the Young People's Band, played cymbals, drums, triangles, and marched to the tune of *Fighting Soldiers*. Afterwards, issued with valve instruments, they learnt their scales, cleaned their silver conches and suffered the mockery of 'Salvation Army all gone barmy.'

The captain commanded the Citadel, situated in the emergency quarter between the pawnbroker and the fire station, brass balls one side, alarm bells the other. He kept his troops on the alert and worked them hard. The Citadel, never left unguarded, used to one hundred per cent capacity, accommodated services and Sunday schools, socials, band and songster practices, prayer meetings and Bible classes. There was no let-up. Weekends, the boys paraded for open air meetings and services in the Citadel morning, noon and night. It was all go. They had no time for mischief. They walked to all parts of the town for the open air meetings, and got to know it like the backs of their hands. Sundays, after morning devotions, they traipsed home for a bite to eat, then traipsed somewhere else. After tea washed, brushed, shoes polished, socks up, spick and span, they paraded again.

Pat and David had cornets. Their tutor, a senior bandsman, old and tired, with wisps of grey hair across his bald head, had enough to do looking after his huge family, but the captain wore him out with these extra duties. Every chance he got he had a snooze. When Pat and David arrived for a lesson he was always hiding having a nap. He taught them simple songs and marches. Where the soprano line divided he favoured David with the melody. Pat resented this and bullied his younger brother all the way home.

At 26 Cheese Row the boys practised in the sunny front room. Andrew had a trombone, George a euphonium. Nell sometimes accompanied the quartet on the piano. Wilmot had to put up with it. He could have left, but stayed. Nell never preached at him, nor tried to save his soul. In spite of the new forces aligned against him, he never changed. Threatened by a whole army, of which Nell and her sons were a well trained contingent, he remained the same old sinner. His fire power still disturbed the house, but, after misdemeanours, Nell softened to his quiet remorse and penitential promises not to offend again. Sobering down after a wild night he would say 'It'll be the workhouse for me, and serves me right.' Nell could not bear the responsibility for such a consequence, so she made excuses for him to stay.

David, as anxious as the others to be rid of Wilmot, had to admit that the old villain sometimes brought him luck. On a country walk with him and Molly he found a gold-crest nest with eggs, a rare prize. Boys in Cheese Row had no conscience about bird eggs. They observed a code not to rag nests nor to take more than one egg. All had shoe box collections without censure from school, parents, police.

David strolled with Wilmot and Molly down the brick path from the scullery door to the outside loo. On the brick boundary wall to the right, the loganberry canes looked strong and vigorous, and the boy dreamed of fresh fruit with milk and sugar, and jam boiling in the saucepan. Freshly shaved, his face red, smooth and shining, Wilmot, in grey flannel army shirt, khaki trousers and braces, admired his birds in the chicken run. 'They look alright,' he said.

His heavy black boots shone in the sun. The flaming red cockerel lorded it over the hens. They scratched in the dust and complained at finding nothing.

'Go and dig some worms,' Wilmot said.

'Will we have the cock for Christmas?' David asked.

'Not if we don't fatten 'im up,' Wilmot said. 'Go and see what you can find.'

On a patch opposite the hen-run Nell struggled to grow chrsyanthemums and Michaelmas daisies. Under their roots David found a worm and poked it through the wire. The cock gobbled it up and glanced sideways with a single eye. Wilmot threw cabbage leaves for the fowl as he went through the wire door into the run to collect the eggs. He gave two to David, one for each hand, smooth and warm. They took the eggs into the house and put them in a dish in the scullery. From the table drawer in the kitchen Wilmot took out an old account book with red covers and, with a small length of indelible pencil, made an entry relating to the egg collection.

'Want to come to the abattoir?' Wilmot asked.

There was no one else in the house. It was Saturday morning, and David had the whole day in front of him. 'Righto,' he said.

On the way to the abattoir David bounced along with a sorbo and left

Wilmot and Molly behind. Near the railway arch a billboard declared
BOVRIL PREVENTS THAT SINKING FEELING. It pictured a happy
looking man in blue striped pyjamas clinging to a Bovril bottle on a
raging sea. David kicked the ball at him. Bang. Bang. Bang. From the
dirt at the bottom of the hoarding a coin rolled onto the pavement.
David grabbed it, scraped it clean and took it to Wilmot. 'Look,' he said.
'I've found a two bob bit.'

Wilmot took the coin, tested it with his teeth, ruffled the top of David's
head. 'Lucky little sod,' he said, and returned the coin.

The abattoir, built into the railway embankment, was dark and noisy
and awash with blood and water. Wilmot selected his trotters from the
heap on the floor and put them in a sack. For a few minutes he talked
race horses and form with one of the butchers.

On the way home Wilmot asked David if he would like to win a
fortune. 'It's your lucky day, ain't it?' he said. 'And there's this 'orse in
the 2.30 . . . Top Hat. A good bet at five to one. With your two bob I'd
win you ten.'

'That's betting,' David said. 'It's against the rules.'

'What rules?'

'Army rules.'

'You're barmy. Nothin' wrong with a little flutter. Better than beggin',
like the bloody Army, always badgerin' to put yer 'and in yer pocket, an'
rattlin' their tins for *War Cry* and self denial an' God knows what. Mark
my words, They'll screw your mother out of every penny she's got.'

It was his favourite taunt. Nell argued that the money was used for
good causes. She knew her facts. The Army went to war with the BEF.
General Booth sent motor ambulances, thirty of them, and ran forty
hostels for troops behind the lines.

When they got back to the house Wilmot lit the copper in the scullery.
When the water boiled he scooped it out with a dipper and poured it into
an old tin bath which he had placed on the brick path near the back door.
He emptied the sack of pigs feet into the boiling water. While the trotters
were soaking he sharpened his cut-throat in the scullery. Then he fetched
himself a chair, and a bowl of cold water to put the trotters in after they
had been scrubbed and shaved. Finally he sat down and started work.
David watched, and listened to the sound of the razor as it scraped the
tough, white skin.

'Well,' said Wilmot. 'D'you want to make some money or don't you?'

'No,' said David. 'I'm going to buy a new ball and some suckers.'

'Sweets,' Wilmot said contemptuously. 'They rots yer teeth. An' balls wears out yer boots. You're wastin' yer money.'

Pat came in. David told him of his good fortune. 'Uncle Jim wants me to put the money on a horse,' he said.

'What horse?' Pat asked.

'Top Hat in the 2.30.'

'I've heard of him,' Pat said. 'He's good.'

'Five to one.'

'Why don't you, then?' asked Pat. 'Think what you could do with that sort of money.'

David had thought, not only of a ball and some sweets, but of a geranium for his mother. The temptation was too great. He handed his money over to Wilmot.

Leaning over the rail of the platform in the Citadel above the penitent form the captain laid down the law in fiery words. On strong drink. 'O God! That men should put an enemy in their mouths to steal away their brains.' On Gambling. 'Some put their trust in chariots, and some in horses; but we will remember the name of the Lord our God.'

Salvationists saved from these evils stood up in the Citadel, made public confession of their sins and testified to the redeeming power of Christ's blood. The most regular testifier was the white haired Elijah, born again drinker, smoker, gambler, wife beater. He glorified in his infirmities and attested to the saving power of the blood of the Lamb. He declared 'Though my sins are as scarlet, I shall be whiter than snow.' Throughout all witness, prayers and addresses he shouted 'Amen' and 'Alleluia' and 'Praise the Lord'. He carried the flag on the march, attended every meeting, Sunday and weekday, and made an exhibition of himself. Every day, winter and summer, he wore the uniform. It was the only outfit he had.

David felt ashamed. The guilt of being a gambler backslider on the road to damnation made him miserable. His mother, out washing floors, had not been there to guide him, and he had not been able to confess to her over the midday meal. In the afternoon he should have helped her with the shopping. Instead, he slid two pennies out of his money box and deserted her to go with Pat to the pictures and drown his sorrows.

That was sinful too, though it was alright to watch the magic lantern. The boys put it on the square yard of landing at the top of the stairs, shut the bedroom doors each side to keep out the light, and projected the slides onto the bulkhead. The oil in the cycle lamp smoked like hell, but the pictures came out full colour, still, silent and innocuous. Not so the black and white movies at the electric picture house across the river. There it was exciting and evil. The Army had no rule book to say so. Nothing was printed in black and white, or cut in stone like the Ten Commandments, but David knew it all the same, and it pricked his conscience as the piano tuned in to the antics of comics and cowboys.

Charlie Chaplin and Ben Turpin mimed jerkily to the moods of the music. Tom Mix and Eddie Polo galloped and stunted to the flickering light. The reels showed Pearl White threatened by grizzlies in abandoned mines. With his companions, David shouted obscenities and swore at the villains who threatened his heroines and heroes. The excitements of the films temporarily banished guilt, but when he came out blinking and squinting in the sun he remembered his offences.

'I wonder how Top Hat got on,' said Pat, and reminded David again of his guilt.

On the way home the brothers wrestled, jumped fences, climbed walls, hung on bars, dagged and dared each other and acted out the antics of the film stars.

Nell, ironing, looked frail and harrassed. Wisps of hair sweated her face. Clomp. Clomp. Clomp. The iron smoothed the clothes. Clang. She banged the iron on the hob for heating again, and picked up another. She was alone. Upstairs, Wilmot snored in a drunken stupor. At the Citadel, George and Andrew chased pretty lasses in bonnets and tunics and black stockings. David entered into his mother's sorrow.

Nell, no zealot, had bought no uniform, and had not joined the Songsters. Of all the accoutrements available she wore only a small Army brooch. Sunday evenings, she put the brooch on her best bright blouse and brushed her hair into a holy light for the service at the Citadel. Under the banner of 'Blood and Fire' she found consolations more precious than those which the pastor had invited her to share with the Rose of Sharon under the Banner of Love. The pastor, who had claimed to be her friend, never visited her. Once she sent Pat and David to his church. The landlord's daughter held their hands and took them in after Sunday school. In the Sung Eucharist Pat made rude remarks and noises concerning smells the boat-boys made with their censors. The two boys could not stop giggling, so they were sent out in disgrace before the sermon.

Nell put away the pile of clothes. 'Come on, boys,' she said. 'You'll be late. Hurry now. Get washed and put your uniforms on.'

The open air meeting outside the Citadel on Saturday evening was for seniors, but juniors went too, and stood on the fringe, listened to the band, the singing, the tambourines and concertinas, and watched the throwing of coins on the drum. It could be exciting. Drunkards from the pub across the road barracked and jeered, like they did at an FA Cup tie at Elm Park.

Pat and David washed at the sink, then changed upstairs. They heard Wilmot snoring. Pat sniffed at the smell of stale cigarette smoke and piss in the po. 'I bet he picked a winner,' he said.

From habit, the boys laid the table for tea. They put out the crockery, the milk and sugar, the butter, a loaf of bread and a pot of jam. Nell had bought macaroons for a treat and asked David to put them on a plate. She cut the bread and butter and made the tea. Her hand trembled as she poured the tea into the cups. The lid chattered to the teapot. The cups chattered to the saucers.

'What's this you've been up to, David?' Nell asked.

'I found a two bob bit,' David said.

'What else did you do?'

'I put a bet on Top Hat.'

'It won,' said his mother. 'Your money is on the mantelpiece.'

'Caw,' exclaimed Pat. 'Isn't he lucky.'

Nell showed no joy in David's good fortune. 'You know it's wrong to bet on horses, don't you?'

'Yes,' said David. 'I'm sorry.'

'What's wrong with it, then?' asked Pat.

'It's getting something for nothing. Taking money you haven't earned is like stealing.'

'Sometimes you lose, mum,' said Pat.

'Then it's money wasted,' said Nell.

'I was going to buy you that geranium,' David said.

'Perhaps. Another time,' Nell said.

'If it were mine I'd buy some new footer boots,' said Pat. 'Twelve bob. That's enough.'

'Twelve shillings! Is that what he should have?' asked Nell.

'Yes,' said Pat.

'There's only a ten shilling note,' Nell said.

'At five to one plus his stake he should get twelve bob,' Pat said.

'He was drunk. That's all he had,' Nell said.

Wilmot had swallowed the stake. Later, when Nell challenged him, he promised to pay David back. The ten shilling note was left on the mantelpiece. David could have taken it, but did not. He hoped his mother would take it and buy a geranium, but she did not. She saw Wilmot look at it with envious eyes when he was broke. The note could not be left there. In the end Nell put it in the Salvation Army Denial envelope.

Chapter 6

For the sake of his mother, David wished to be a paragon, a little white dove goody-goody like Miss Alice, but failed, went to movies and football matches, and smoked dog-ends and herbal cigarettes in secret. It troubled him when the captain declared that God knew everything, even when you tried to keep things dark. It was scary, someone knowing all your secrets. When he felt guilty he sometimes went to the mercy seat and confessed his sins to the Sunday school teacher. Pat did not mind who knew about his indiscretions. He used to talk to Wilmot about betting. 'Life is a gamble,' Wilmot said. Pat agreed.

One girl is born a beauty, another has buck teeth. Of a hundred horses in the stable, only one wins the Derby. David, in the race for ten-year-olds, came fifth in a field of forty-three. The trainer said his form was very good, he showed promise and should do well. He found arithmetic hard going, tried hard, but ended up a back marker. The history and geography punters thought he should have been better placed. The lady trainer in geography fancied his mapwork and gave him a prize, Charles Dickens' *Tale of Two Cities*. Sidney Carton, that sad loser, became a firm favourite with David who, at English, found the going to his liking. His trainer said he showed a great interest in literature, grammar and composition. He proved a front runner at handwriting, but fell back at spelling. His behaviour was very good, and he was pulled up only once for detention.

In the hurdle of selection for secondary education, George, Andrew and Pat jumped clear and qualified. Pat took to electrics and went in for cat's whisker wireless stuff, but nearly lost everything when he tripped and fell into the whirlpools of the lock. George and Andrew rescued him and became heroes to young ladies in army bonnets dreaming of motherhood and seeking brave men to whom they could teach gifts of tenderness and love. Wearying of their mother's solemn rigours, George and Andrew looked for a lighter, smiling, indulgent feminity.

The postman brought a brown paper parcel for George.

'This is it,' he told his mother, and quickly opened it to find the first volume of *The Peoples of All Nations*. He looked proud. Nell and his brothers smiled admiringly.

George, now a printer like his father, had the same short, chunky build. His smile broadened, showed his even, Jersey milk teeth as he thumbed through the pages. With his first wages he bought a bike on easy payments to save tram fares to his work on the other side of town. When the bike was paid for he subscribed to the weekly magazine which he had bound in stiff, red covers lettered in gold. He handed the book to his mother.

'It's lovely,' Nell said.

'This is only the first,' George said. He did not have his father's curls. His tufty hair fell straight from a parting at the side across a broad forehead and over his ears.

'How many more, then?' Pat asked.

'Twelve altogether. One every month,' George said.

Each boy inspected the book. It was like a new window opening on the world, showing lands of earthquake, volcano, hurricane, famine and flood, and paradises of sea and silver sand and palm trees in the sun. There was a whole world of wonder out there waiting to be discovered. From camp with the Boys Brigade on the Isle of Wight George had brought back a bottle of coloured sand. It stood on the kitchen mantelpiece, a little bit of earth's magic. He also bought a volume of Tennyson's poems. At secondary school he had played a thief in *Ali Ba Ba* and become acquainted with Scheherezade in *The Tales of the Arabian Nights*. George in long trousers, on the threshold of manhood, was ready for girls.

Nell on the piano accompanied her quartet of bandsmen in the front room; George on the euphonium, Andrew the trombone, and Pat and David each with cornets. They reached the end of *Rockingham*.

...Love so amazing, so divine,
Demands my soul, my life, my all.

'Very good,' Nell said, 'I am proud of you.'

She rose from the piano. David took her place and stumbled through the largo of *Won't you buy my pretty flowers* in the Smallwood's primary.

Pat nagged. 'What an awful noise,' he said. 'Let Andrew have a go.'

Andrew, more like Nell, darker than George, had started work at an engineering firm. He was doing well. His boss invited him to a Christmas party and sent back a box of chocolates for Nell. Andrew took great care of his appearance, used brilliantine on his hair and brushed it back off the forehead and over his ears. He hated braces and always wore a belt. He was the pianist of the family. Nell had taught them all the simple scales, then, out of her meagre resources, paid a teacher to give them lessons.

Andrew, smart and fresh in a clean shirt, collar with a pin, and a coloured tie, sat at the piano and played *Robin's Return*. Then, with great élan, he played the frantic, semi-quaver ridden *Maiden's Prayer*.

'My word,' said Nell. 'You are doing well.'

Salvation Army lasses, with curls under their bonnets, were waiting for him at the Citadel. He too was ready for girls.

Life was getting easier for Nell. George and Andrew were working, bringing in a little money, and Pat was established at secondary school. That left David. She saw an advertisement in the local newspaper inviting applications to sit scholarships for Sivier's, a three-hundred-year-old foundation for fatherless boys. 'I think you would stand a chance,' she told David, and filled up the form.

When David passed the exam, the headmaster at his junior school made him stand on a chair so that everyone could see him, like a statue on a pedestal. After school his mates called him a shit. At Sivier's he would wear green stockings the colour of cow-pat.

News of David's success spread round the Citadel and gave his family a little kudos. In the army hierarchy, at the lowest level, ex-convicts and rotters of all sorts strove against former sin, their staying power always in doubt. Those who survived became flag-wavers, flaunted long service stripes and lorded it over the poor wretches still floundering in the slough of sin. Above them, Salvationists from birth became non-commisssioned officers and Sunday school teachers. Some of them joined the officer class and became corps commanders, even staff officers and commissioners at London HQ and Regent's Hall. Highest of all, the General and his family, children of William Booth the founder. The Booths were seldom seen, but much reported in *The War Cry*.

Diana, daughter of the captain, corps commander of Reading I Citadel, attended Sunday school like everyone else. In a room no bigger than a badminton court, boys and girls fidgeted and turned their heads in search of something more interesting than the prayer, the song, the teacher's spiel. In an exchange of glances David and Diana found each other in the old eye game. She, a young Hebe with a longish face set in a cluster of dark ringlets to her shoulders, had bright, liquid, shimmering eyes which reminded David of those river shallows in the sun, dancing with the colours of trees and flowers. Other boys came under her spell, including Pat, who had the advantage of an association with her brother John. The two friends were building a crystal set. Pat and David often competed for the same prize, but for Diana, Pat never had a chance, not having that dreamy, brown eyed curly look which the young goddess saw in David.

Having started with an exchange of short, shy glances in Sunday school, it developed in the services. They eyed each other from opposite sides of the Citadel, Diana in Junior Songsters facing David in the Young People's Band. After services, David hung about the big swing doors and waited for Diana's departure with the captain's family, content only to look, knowing he could not speak. Other times, leaving early with Nell, knowing Diana had not yet gone, he looked back until he reached the street corner under the pawnbroker's brass balls, beyond which there was no possibility of seeing her again until the next event at the Citadel.

It seemed an unlikely match. Nell, a new entrant, must have given the impression of being half-hearted. She wore no uniform, came and went quietly, with some dignity, had no conviction of sin and showed no contrition at the penitent form. The captain would hardly have noticed her had not someone recommended her to do his laundry. So there was a divide; Diana in the ruling class, David the son of the washerwoman. It did not stop them making eyes, then exchanging notes.

'Dear Diana,' David wrote, 'will you be my sweetheart?'

David watched the note pass along the row, saw the blush of her smile as she read it, and, when they trooped out, touched her hand. From then on they could not keep their eyes off each other. David hated the intervals when they were apart.

Nell had delayed writing to Miss Alice at Hambleden, but finally sent a letter to which the lady replied that she would love to meet, and could Nell bring David who had made such an impression on her sister Miss Celia at Richmond.

In the Easter holidays Nell and David caught an afternoon bus to Henley where Miss Alice met them in an old, green, open four-seater Wolseley. The two women hugged each other. Miss Alice shook David by the hand.

'Jump in,' Miss Alice said, and offered David a seat in the back under the folded canvas hood. Nell took the front passenger seat and slammed the door. Miss Alice slid into the driver's seat on the side with the spare wheel and the horn.

'My word, this is a thrill, isn't it, David?' Nell said.

Pretty Miss Alice, dark and slim, wore a red silk scarf tied in a knot at the back of her head. As she belted round the narrow, winding lanes, the scarf trailed in the breeze and brushed David's face. The breeze blew in at the sides. Nell had to hold her hat.

They turned into a long, gravel drive and stopped opposite the entrance porch of a large, red brick house. The house had two gables at the front, each with two large bays, upstairs and downstairs. The huge garden, with wide lawns, stretched down to the river where there was a brick boat-house. Miss Alice, a younger, more lively version of Miss Celia, told David to run off and play with the children, then took Nell by the arm and led her up the stone steps to the porch and into the house.

There were children everywhere, in light, coloured casuals, playing ball and skipping games. Nell had done a good job on David, fresh and clean, his boots polished, but the other children ignored him, and he felt out of place in his hand-me-downs. The boys and girls called each other by name. David identified Sybil and Connie, Miss Celia's girls, whose photos he had seen in the big house at Richmond.

A ball came rolling at David's feet. He was about to kick it when a small boy came running and picked it up.

'Who are you?' the small boy asked.

'David Sedgewick.'

'Oh, I know, the poor little orphan. Mummy told us about you.'

Voices called impatiently. 'Throw the ball.' The small boy threw the ball and ran away.

David wandered off and sat by the river near the boat-house. Two men and their girls came in a punt, pulled in at the landing stage, moored the boat and walked arm-in-arm to the house.

Miss Alice and a maid arranged a picnic on the grass. Miss Alice and Nell sat together and talked. It seemed to David that they were enjoying themselves, and he was glad, though he felt excluded and a little jealous. He sat next to Sybil, quieter than Connie and the rest of the children. She looked after him and kept him supplied with food. She was older than David, and had thick, kinky, fair hair and blue eyes. He liked her. She joined the others in a riot of laughter and chatter. He felt a spectator.

In the bus going home Nell drew close to David and hugged him. 'Phew,' she exclaimed. 'I had forgotten Miss Alice had so many sisters. All those children. You must have got lost in the crowd.'

Throughout the afternoon David consoled himself with the thought of Diana, and longed to see her again at the Citadel.

Nell, anxious about herself and the future of her boys, began to plan ahead, and formed a scheme centred on Phoebe, a bonnet and tunic Army girl who, with her black woollen stockings, wore sensible flat shoes. Phoebe, without a family, alone in the world, worked as a domestic at one of the big houses on the Oxfordshire side of the Thames at Caversham. She had made herself known to Nell who saw her as a paragon. Plain, yes, but none the worse for that, and a good soul-mate for George. Nell's emergency scheme was that, if anything happened to her, Phoebe would take over her woman's role and make George a good, practical partner and look after him. She hinted at these things to her protegee, who guessed the strategem, sought Nell out at the Citadel, and, by gaining favour, attempted to endear herself to George by this indirect approach. Who could blame Phoebe for that? She could only make her way in the world by following up her chances.

Saturday afternoon Phoebe helped Nell with the shopping. When they got back she started the ironing.

'Aren't I lucky, David?' Nell said. 'Here is Phoebe doing all my work. Isn't it kind of her?'

Phoebe stayed for tea. Everyone was on their best behaviour. Wilmot, drousy from lunchtime drinking, took Phoebe out into the garden to look at the hens. When they came back Phoebe cut the bread and butter, put out the cake, spooned out the jam. Nell came with the tea.

'Now, my dear,' Nell said to Phoebe, 'you sit here next to George.' To George she said, 'Now, George, pull up a chair for Phoebe.'

The two women monopolised the conversation, mostly culinary and domestic. Nell drew out Phoebe's accomplishments for George's benefit, and, between talk of pastries, puddings and preserves, pressed him into attentiveness.

'Help Phoebe to bread and butter, George.'

'Phoebe, have some jam. George will pass it to you.'

'Now, Phoebe, what about some cake? Cut it for her, George.'

Highly coloured, large nosed, charmless and plain, Phoebe sat back, clasped her hands in her lap, enjoyed the fuss, and beamed shyly whenever Nell cajoled her son into politeness.

Wilmot guessed what was afoot and started mischief. 'They tell me you're in lodgings,' he said to Phoebe.

'Yes, with an old widow woman at Whitley.'

'That's a long way from your work,' said Wilmot.

'I catch a tram to the bridge and walk from there.'

'You ought to get a bit nearer. Save the tram fares.'

Phoebe deepened colour, as though Wilmot had caught her out in some foolish extravagance.

'Does she feed you well?' asked Wilmot.

Phoebe fidgeted with embarrassment and looked to Nell for support.

'Phoebe isn't very satisfied,' Nell said. 'The old lady is a Salvationist and a widow. She only has her little bit of pension, and needs the money. Phoebe doesn't like to leave her.'

Wilmot exploded. 'Salvationists. They're all the same. They're all after your money. It's all they damn well think about. A man can't 'ave a quiet drink without them badgerin' you with coin bags. If it ain't money for *The War Cry* it's money for self denial.'

Phoebe, hot as the sun, turned deepest red.

'Take no notice,' Nell said, and trembled with anxiety not to allow the situation to get out of control.

'Why don't you let 'er come an' live 'ere, missus? You're a poor widow in need of the money. What's more, the best cook in town. She'd get fed 'ere alright.'

George, even tempered, easy-going, coming up to manhood, needed to prove himself. For the sake of peace he had tolerated Wilmot's indiscretions. Now he was directly affected. He had seen through his mother's strategems. As things were, he could handle the problem. But there had been a woman boarder before. His mother might take Wilmot's idea seriously. The strain of Phoebe under the same roof would be unbearable. He had to do something to stop it. 'Shut up, you old devil,' he shouted.

Wilmot, a giant compared with George, glared. 'Watch yer tongue, boy. I'll tan the 'ide off you.' He softened his tone. 'Anyway, I'd a thought you'd want yer sweetheart 'ere. Wouldn't you, missus?'

'Be quiet, you silly old fool,' Nell said.

The goitre on her throat was growing into a gigantism. She tried to pour a cup of tea. The chatter of china sounded like a death rattle. The palsy forced her to put down the pot. David stood up and finished the pouring for her.

George bit his lip, nailed it against further aggravation of the lodger.

Wilmot would not be denied. 'What's the matter, then?' he challenged. 'Don't you love 'er? Got someone else, 'ave you?'

George remembered the girl he really cared for, sweet and dark and starry eyed, and not a bit like Phoebe.

'I thought so,' said Wilmot, and turned to Phoebe, 'Don't you bother with 'im, my gal. 'E don't deserve you. You're too good for 'im. Go an' find yerself a nice boy. Let 'im ruin 'imself on a pretty face.'

Phoebe burst into tears and ran into the scullery. George rushed round the table to Wilmot. Andrew followed in support, but Nell lifted an arm to bar their way.

'Get out of here,' George shouted. 'Go on, get out.'

Pat joined his brothers in a triple alliance against the enemy. Wilmot rose and retreated. David got up from his seat against the wall and let him through. At the door to the passage Wilmot uttered a last threat. 'You wait, you bloody little whippersnappers. I'll get you.' He raised his fist before opening the door to go upstairs. After a few minutes he came down, called Molly, slammed the door and went out.

Phoebe recovered composure, dried her eyes and asked for her bonnet. Nell took her upstairs. The four boys cleared the table and washed up. Phoebe came down ready to go.

'We'll come with you,' George said.

George and Andrew fetched their instruments and left with Phoebe.

The issues had come into the open. Nell, too eager to see the fruit of her labour, had attempted to constrain her eldest son to a disciplined largo. He, in the spring of life, desired the swift dance of allegro. Things could never be the same.

Nell calmed and prettied herself. In the street she linked arms with Pat and David, and they marched uphill to the Citadel. It was the eve of Pentecost. The Holy Ghost was on his way.

Whit Sunday saw David desolate without Diana. Services at the Citadel were taken by a surrogate from Wales. At the end of the day, after a fiery sermon, he sweated blood to get sinners to the penitent form.

'Who'll be the first?' the surrogate shouted from behind the rail of the platform. In support, behind him, a whole phalanx of uniformed warrant officers, bonneted Songsters and the Senior Band.

Lead, kindly Light, amid the encircling gloom,
Lead thou me on;
The night is dark, and I am far from home;
Lead thou me on.
Keep thou my feet; I do not ask to see
The distant scene; one step enough for me.

The Band played, the Songsters sang softly, pleadingly. One or two of the congregation left their seats, walked with bowed heads, clasped hands, and knelt at the mercy seat. The preacher leaned over the rail and welcomed them. Long-serving, trusted Salvationists knelt beside the penitents and listened to their confessions. The Welshman, in earnest prayer, closed his eyes, looked up to heaven, lifted his arms to God and implored his forgiveness for those who had responded to the call. He importuned others to relieve themselves of the burden of sin. 'Who'll be the next?' he shouted.

Backsliders who, during the week, had smoked, drunk a glass of beer, placed a bet, been to a theatre or cinema, tormented with guilt, went sobbing, broken with remorse, to the penitent form. David watched from the body of the hall where he sat with his mother. Phoebe left the Songsters on the platform, walked down the steps and knelt at the mercy seat. The surrogate captain, on this day of Pentecost had to achieve a full bench of sinners, and give a good report to Diana's father when he came back. 'God is speaking to you,' he declared. 'Listen and be saved. Take the first frail step. Come to him.'

David shared his mother's song book, which shook with her hand. Phoebe did not return to the platform, but came to sit the other side of Nell. Shame and self reproach behind her, now calm and reconciled, her frustrated fantasies banished in the emotion of contrition, Phoebe hugged Nell's arm. On the other side of David, Pat fidgeted, anxious to be away. George played with the Senior Band on the platform. Andrew, in the darkness of the overhead balcony at the back of the hall, talked and joked quietly with friends, and with lasses in bonnets and tunics and black stockings.

Diana and her family were back for the corps outing to Goring on Whit Monday. For this innocent excursion the Salvationists had left their uniforms behind. All except Elijah were dressed in bright civilian clothes. The coach followed the road through Pangbourne, then along the river to the railway bridge and under the trees to the point where the Thames cuts through the chalk of the Chilterns. At The Bull the party filed out into a fine spring day. Turning left off the road the trippers lifted their eyes to the hills and, by a rough track, climbed the steep escarpment in front of them.

David, now sturdy in patched, washed trousers, new grey socks and laced, black boots made straight for Diana. His inspiration was there in front of him, not at the top of the hill. How neat and pretty she looked in her green woollen dress, her short white socks and brown buttoned shoes. Side by side, after a few paces they pretended to make hard work of climbing the hill. They laughed at each other, bent backed, hands on hips, legs wide apart, their bodies swinging from side to side. Her eyes sparkled. With the exaggerated movements her shining dark hair flopped about the white collar of her dress. The skirt of her dress flounced and swirled like a Scottish kilt. She held out her hand. David grabbed it and felt the innocence of the little white cuffs against the green of her frock.

Nell struggled with Phoebe and laughed at their antics. Pat raced to the front with Diana's brother.

At the top of the hill there was a sudden dispersal. David and Diana went wild with brambles, grew tender under trees and gambolled on the grass.

'Catch me,' Diana demanded.

They ran with the breeze, met tangentially, then parted, like warblers mating on the wing.

'Watch this,' David said, and showed her a cartwheel and a handstand. His reward, her smile, was more acceptable than silver coins along the river.

'Look. A fairy-ring. Let's dance,' Diana said, and pointed to the grass.

They held hands at arms lenth and swung into the circle. Afterwards they found daisies for chains, buttercups for golden kisses. Children and grown-ups crowded. The pair were hardly ever alone. yet always alone, conscious only of each other.

The idyll ended. Smelling of earth, trees, flowers, they hung back, closed together and talked.

'Where is Wolverhampton?' Diana asked.

'Up north somewhere,' David said.

'Even I know that,' Diana teased.

'I think it's in the Black Country.'

'Ugh. It sounds horrid.'

'Why do you want to know?'

'Mummy and daddy were talking. We've got to go there.'

The news, like distant thunder, threatened, but could not spoil the day.

'D'you mean you're going there to live?'

'Yes,' Diana said sadly.

'For good?'

'I suppose so, until we're moved again.'

'When do you go?'

'September, I think.'

'That's when I go to my new school.'

'Slimy socks,' she teased, and laughed, and ran ahead for David to chase her to the coach. They took seats on opposite sides of the gangway and waited for their parents.

Nell, in her woollen skirt and purple striped blouse, came first, small and slim, but blooming. Wisps of brown hair trailed across her face. She sat with David. He felt the quivering warmth of her body. 'My word, David, you've had a good old romp,' she said.

'It's been spiffiing,' David said. 'How about you?'

'Lovely. A lovely day,' Nell said, and pressed her boy's knee with her trembling hand.

The innocent romance, nothing the parents needed to worry about, bloomed all summer, thriving with urgent notes passed along the rows, telling each other where and when, but on August Bank Holiday weekend, when the corps went on a coach trip to Southsea, Diana and her family went the other way, to Wolverhampton.

On a sunless, miserable day, David sat with his mother on the hard, cold pebbles of the beach. On that Saturday afternoon the hostile wind blew with a wet stickiness as they ate their sandwiches. No one wanted to bathe. David gazed at the sea, a strange new element. The pebbles danced with the ebb and flow of the surf. Waves reared angrily, tossing spumes of spray, reminding him of pictures he had seen in *The Peoples of All Nations*; black Africans with plumes and spears stamping out a war dance. The sea was like that, full of menace.

Nell and her family lodged with the local Salvationists. That night, David developed a fever and had a nightmare. Sunday, his mother made him stay in bed. Monday, they went home.

The following Saturday, David, fully recovered, delivered the captain's laundry. Diana and her brother John had been left under the eye of a neighbour. When David arrived, hot and sweaty from the long walk with the heavy bundle, Pat was already in the house, working with John in their search for the secrets of the cat's whisker. John let him in, then rushed back to the crystal set.

The terrace house had the same plan and accommodation as the one in Cheese Row, but with the distinction of a porch and a bay window at the front.

David followed John into the kitchen. 'Where's Diana?' he asked.

'Upstairs, somewhere,' John said without bothering to look up, absorbed in his hobby with Pat.

David dumped the bundle and rushed upstairs. The window of Diana's room faced east. The sun had passed over. Her bedroom had become a cool and shaded sanctuary. David sat beside her on the bed and held her hand. He, in his shirt, looked shabby beside her, cool in gingham.

'What's this I've been hearing about you?' Diana asked.

'It's been awful without you, 'David said.

'Fancy going to the seaside and being ill.'

'It wasn't anything serious. The nightmare was the worst.'

'Tell me about it.'

'We were in this castle with high, stone walls. Arrows came whizzing down on us. We sheltered under the ramparts. An arrow came flying straight at my mother. I thought it was going to kill her. Then I woke up in a sweat.'

'You're sweating now,' Diana said.

'It's nice and cool in here. You're lucky having a bedroom all to yourself.'

'I'd like a swim.'

'Where?'

'The Baths. They're quite near.'

'I like the river. We ought to go one day.'

'I don't like the river. Mummy and daddy say it's dirty. They say it's dangerous.'

'Pat nearly drowned. George and Andrew rescued him from the lock. The weeds are dangerous. You can get tangled up.'

'That's what daddy says. You be careful. I'm not coming with you.'

'You'd be alright. I'd look after you.'

'Boys do silly things. How's John and Pat getting on with that silly old crystal set. Does it work yet?'

'I don't know. I came straight upstairs.'

'John's silly. Months he's been working on it. He says he'll be able to hear people in America.'

'That's a long way.'

'So is Wolverhampton.'

'Perhaps we could talk to each other on the crystal set.'

'Silly,' Diana said, and laughed.

'I found it on the map.' David said, 'it's near Birmingham. It's got a good footer team. Wolverhampton Wanderers. They're in the First Division.'

'I don't want to go.'

'Don't you like it there?'

'It's awful. It's in the Black Country, like you said.'

'Perhaps it won't be so bad.'

'I shan't know anyone.'

'You'll be alright. You'll soon make friends.'

'That's what mummy says, but my friends are here. I don't want any new ones.'

'It's exciting, seeing new places. Mum took us to Isleworth, That's near London. We went to Richmond Park. Our school took us to Wembley Empire Exhibition. We saw the cowboys. I didn't like Southsea much.'

'How far is it?'

'Where? Southsea?'

'No, silly. Wolverhampton.'

'Too far to walk. I should think it's about one hundred miles.'

'That's a long way,' Diana said sadly.

'Too far to bring the washing,' David said, trying to cheer her up. Diana withdrew her hand. 'P'raps there'll be some nice boys there.'

'Like me, you mean.'

'Better than you.'

A sudden jealousy added to the pain David felt at her departure. 'You won't find a better sweetheart than me,' he said.

'I don't believe you like me a bit,' Diana said.

David took back her hand and kissed it. Then he remembered the things he had meant to say, and guessed they were the things she wanted to hear. 'Wolverhampton is like the end of the world,' he said. 'Why do they have to take you away? I don't want you to go. I want you to stay here. Then we could grow up together and be real sweethearts. I'll miss you. We may never see each other again.'

Diana kissed his sweaty cheek. He looked into her eyes. Those coloured pools he loved so much were full of tears. He could not plumb their depths. His enchantment, tinged with fear, precluded speech. Suddenly, awkwardly, they collapsed into each other's arms and relaxed in an ecstacy of innocent joy. For a few moments of timeless wonder they held each other in a dream of the afternoon.

Pat recalled them to reality. 'Come on, David. It's time we went.' he shouted.

Chapter 7

Life seemed full of mystery; under the conjuror's diamante cloth; in glistening grass, sparkling water, the rainbow in the sky. To search out secrets David dug into clay banks, picked flower petals, flew kites in the wind, and dived into river weeds. He found nothing. Seeking his mother's mystery in the sheets of her bed, nothing was revealed except the sweet scent of her body and clothes. What was the magic in Diana's eyes? By some strange chance they were thrown together on the same shore. Pebbles danced and they were lifted to a crest of a wave, then lost to each other on the fall.

Diana went her way, David his, to Sivier's with the motto *Magna est Veritas at Prevalet*. Great is Truth and It Prevails. The school, three hundred years old, with its books and teachers, would know everything, the wisdom of the ages. No more secrets. No more mysteries. 'I am proud of you,' Nell said. 'Be sure and be a good boy and learn all you can.'

She took him to the outfitters and bought him a cap, a tie and a pair of socks in grey and green.

'What's all the fuss?' asked Pat.

Nell took David to have a look at the school before the first day of term. They found a large Victorian house standing well back from the road near Pig's Green. The simple dignity of its front had only one architectural extra, a portico entrance with a pair of painted Sivier boy figures in full uniform, one each side of the portico at roof level. A fine cedar, taller than the house, between the two drives from the road, symbol of prosperity and longevity, spread its branches like the blessing of a black robed priest.

'What a lovely tree,' Nell said. 'You are a lucky boy, and no mistake.'

She saw the friendly front as a backcloth to a stage on which David had been called to play a part. In reality the front was a façade, out of bounds to the pupils except on Sundays when the boarders marched out along one of the drives to St. Edmund's in the town. Otherwise scholars went in and out past lavatories and garden sheds via the tradesman's entrance, a narrow gate to a side street on the eastern boundary of the school.

Under the terms of the Founder's will, Trustees were appointed to find an honest Godly man to educate twenty poor male children in reading, writing and ciphering, and teach them the Catechism in the points of the Christian religion. Sivier's, which started in a pub, had progressed to the Victorian residence, but, sick with poverty, it struggled to keep itself alive, having to pay twentieth century bills with nineteenth century rents from Trust properties.

The teaching parts, humble and inadequate, comprised the long upper room of a large building at the back of and at right angles to the Victorian house. The two structures formed an L, of which the school building was the longer arm, stairs led up to the fourth and fifth forms. The teachers of these two forms faced each other, one each end of the long room, and fought for the attention of their respective pupils in the space between. A pupil in one form, bored by the lesson, could listen to the teacher of the other form for something more to his taste. A glass partition separated the so-called sixth form from the lower classes.

At ground level, the hat and coat lobby gave access to a room which served three purposes; a stationary store, the tuck-shop, and a place where the headteacher delivered pandies. In this bittersweet room David received a caning in his first year when he still enjoyed the fun of talking to his neighbours. Nell wormed it out of him when she saw him holding his bottom. 'There is a time for talking, and there is a time for keeping quiet,' she said. 'You will learn.'

A green painted corrugated iron covered way followed the inside angle of the L from the hat and coat lobby, and gave access to the boarder's dining room, called the buttery, though it stored no wine, the carpentry shop, the new lavatory block and dorms, and, along the back of the Victorian house, the staff common room, the headmaster's private quarters, and the kitchens. At the end of the covered way, a gibbet-like structure supported the school bell.

The lawn in the angle of the L was out of bounds. Beyond the lawn to the north, boys kicked out their shoes in a large gravel play area enclosed by high, prison-like walls.

Of the hundred or so pupils, about thirty were boarders. The school had an atmosphere of hostility, between boarders and day boys, seniors and juniors, Foundation scholarship boys and Non-Foundationers, staff and boys, headmaster and staff. It was an Alma Mater without benefit of femininity.

David's conceit at winning a scholarship took a jolt at the outset when studying the noticeboard to trace his name in all the lists; House lists, sports lists, duty lists, all new to him. Small for his age, he stretched on tiptoe to read them all. Senior boys, like giants, surrounded him. One of them, a boarder, lifted him up from behind, stuck his nose in the lists and said 'There you are, Jun, now you can see.' His companions laughed, and he dropped David who, deflated and despised as lowest of the low, crept away under a crowd of strange, intimidating toughs in grey corduroy breeches with silver side buttons, green stockings up to their thighs, and dark grey jerseys.

To get to Sivier's, the other side of town, too far to walk, David caught a tram to Turnpike terminus, then walked half a mile to the school. Tom Selborne from across the river caught the same tram. The two boys rushed upstairs to the open top, claimed front seats and watched the sparks fly as the cable arm trailed the overhead wires.

The school day started with prayers in the large schoolroom; a hymn, six verses of a Psalm, the Collect and an Our Father, and Bible readings set by the Church Calendar. Then school lessons until 12.50 with a mid-morning break. David and Tom took sandwiches for lunch, but often shared them with each other and with overbearing boarders, hungry and scrounging food. Afternoon lessons started at 2.00 and ended at 3.30. Then it was home, or games in the public park up the road, football in winter, cricket in summer. Wednesday afternoon was a holiday made up by working Saturday morning.

There was no system of fagging, but senior boarders used junior day boys to take home dirty linen and empty tuck boxes; also to deliver letters to girlfriends, and buy fags from the former tuck-shop in the side street, which had lost its status as a reprisal for selling contraband. David performed duties for a boarder whose mother was a widow and lived in a street which led off Cheese Row opposite his junior school. The house was another terrace, but with a small bay window showing a geranium, and a bigger garden. David felt his status to be lower. The mother gave him tips, but never asked him in, nor showed any interest in his personal circumstances. David was never asked to do anything which would have got either him or his taskmaster into trouble, but the parcels, often heavy and cumbersome, became a nuisance when added to a satchel of books and homework.

Between tram and home David suffered molestation by lads from his old school. The ruffians would set about him, knock the parcels out of his hand, pull his satchel, throw away his school hat.

'Goodness, David, what have you been up to?' Nell would ask when she saw him awry.

David confided.

Nell hugged him. 'You have to be brave,' she would say. 'Life is a struggle, and no mistake.'

Wednesdays, for lunch, Nell baked the boy a steak and kidney pie because she knew it was his favourite.

Towards the end of David's first summer term at Sivier's, the doctor ordered Nell to hospital, the only place she could be made to rest and get proper treatment.

'How can I go to hospital?' she complained to David. 'Who would look after you?'

'What about Aunt Tilly?' David asked. 'Wouldn't she help?'

'She's done so much already. I don't like asking her.'

'She wouldn't mind. She's nice.'

He was right, Nell thought. Tilly would do anything.

'We'll go and see her,' Nell said. 'Give ourselves a treat. You like it out there, don't you? I'll get all my work done and take you Saturday afternoon. Pat can come too,'

The red, single decker bus bumped them along to Aunt Tilly's cottage at Peppard in the Chilterns. *Peacehaven*, of brick, rough cast and tile, one of a pair in a row of six, had a good, big garden with a wide space at the side. House-martins welcomed summer visitors at the door.

Tilly Westmoreland stirred the embers of her kitchen range fire, fed them with a handful of twigs from the yard, and pressed a kettle of water on the blaze. 'Well, boys, what have you been up to?' she enquired, really wanting to know, and waiting for an answer before setting the table for tea. 'How's school, Pat?'

'Not so bad. I'm building a crystal set.'

'Are you, by Jove. I've heard about them. Do they really work?'

'Mine will. I'm going to listen to America.'

'I can't believe it,' Aunt Tilly said with mock seriousness.

'You'll see,' said Pat, and laughed.

Aunt Tilly laid the cloth. Nell fetched crockery from the drainer in the scullery.

'What about you, David? How's the new school?'

'Not so bad,' said David.

'He's doing very well,' Nell said. 'I've brought his last school report for you to see.'

Pat, not wishing to hear, resentful of the attention his younger brother was getting, rushed out to play with Tilly's children, Hatty and Harry.

Nell, though careful not to embarrass the boy, liked to tell people how well he was doing at his new school. She did it in her own quiet way, in answer to questions, not like a publicity agent, pushing him forward. With palsied hands she found the fullscap envelope in her handbag and gave it to her friend.

Tilly read the report aloud. 'Position in Form – 1. Number in Form – 30. Has done exceedingly well.' Then she counted eight first places, five seconds, one third, a tenth in geography and a thirteenth in arithmetic. 'My word,' she said, 'you're a bright button and no mistake. I should think you're very proud of him, Nell.'

'He couldn't have done better could he?' Nell said, and, shaking nervously, fumbled the report back into the envelope and into her handbag.

David enjoyed these soft words, and the smell of wood smoke from the fire. He would like to have played in the garden, but, sensitive to Pat's teasing, stayed with the women.

'What about you, gal?' Tilly asked, and, from her seat near the fire, looked searchingly at Nell.

'As you see, still shaking like a leaf,' Nell said.

'What does the doctor say?'

'The same old thing. Rest, he tells me.'

'She's got to go into hospital,' David said.

'I wasn't going to worry you about that,' Nell said. 'After all, George and Andrew are big enough to look after themselves.'

'What about Pat and David?' Tilly asked.

'I'm hoping my brothers will have them. Just for the holidays,' Nell said, but could not hide her uncertainty.

'Let them come here,' Tilly said. She stopped buttering the bread, and waved the greasy knife aloft to show the extent of her bounty. Her red hair flamed and licked her face. With a draught of inspiration her friendship flared.

'You've got enough to do,' Nell said. 'I can't ask you again.'

'What are friends for?' said Tilly.

'Bless you,' Nell said, knowing the inadequacy of words to express her emotion, and remembering the lean years of the war when her friend gave her surpluses of food from the hotel larder. Tilly, as always, had an abundance at her disposal. Nell, reluctant to depend on others, even her best friend, for the care of her children, sobbed at the realisation of her inadequacy. She dabbed her eyes and recovered composure.

'That's settled then,' said Tilly, and went on to discuss the arrangements. David would go to Isleworth for a week while Pat went camping at Hastings. Then they would both go to Tilly for the rest of the holidays.

The women relaxed.

'Isn't the country lovely?' Nell said.

'Let's have some tea, then we'll go for a walk,' Tilly said.

David called the other children.

'Go and fetch your dad,' Tilly told Harry, and he rushed across the road to the village Memorial Hall where his father was playing bowls.

Harry Westmoreland came in with his son and joined the others at the tea table. One large plate had bread and butter, and another had a pile of Tilly's home made scones. From the two pound jam jar she scooped out large dollops of her own lemon curd and plastered it on the children's bread. Then there was cake.

After tea Uncle Harry attempted a quick exit to the bowling green, but changed his mind when Aunt Tilly niggled him about his weekly chores. He chauffered a Harley Street doctor who had a cottage on the other side of the Common. The two men returned from London on Friday evenings and went back Monday morning. The weekend was the only time Uncle Harry had to cultivate the big back garden, full of fruit and vegetables. In her role as bountiful mother, Tilly saw to it that her cornucopia stayed full.

With a laugh and a show of fine white teeth Uncle Harry dodged his duties as long as possible, but, in the end, Aunt Tilly, twice his size, bullied him into compliance. With a song, he went off to dig the garden, unlock the flaps of the well, water the crops, clean out the chemical closet, chop wood, and trim the oil lamps in the house. For every job undone he made an excuse that he had no time. He would do it next week.

'You want your head examined,' Aunt Tilly told him. 'Get a job round here. Then you'd have time.'

Her husband put his arm round her, pulled her to him with a laugh, kissed the wisps of red hair on her cheek, then deserted her for his cronies across the road.

'Ah well, they have to have their fun,' said Aunt Tilly. 'Let's go for our walk.'

Across the field leading to Spring Woods Nell enthused over the countryside. Her thoughts turned to the past, to Jersey, and her rambles with Jack when they were first married. 'We walked miles and miles that summer before George was born. Then, when he came in the spring, Jack was so proud of his baby son, and carried him everywhere.'

'I bet he did,' said Tilly, 'I can imagine. I should think he burst his tunic.'

'I shall never forget when George was born,' Nell said. 'Jack brought daffodils and put them in an old cracked jug. I can still remember that room at the farm – roses on the walls, the white ceiling, the orange pattern lino, that jug with the daffodils, the sun shining on the red mahogany, the blue linen beadspread. I pulled down the shawl from George's face and Jack said he wasn't as handsome as him, but he would be alright as long as he was like his mother in all his ways. Then he bent over and kissed us. He was redder than the sun, and bigger, like a giant in that tunic with his stripes and his medal and his buttons shining like gold.'

'There's nothing better than having babies,' Tilly said.

'George was easy. Our troubles came later when Jack was leaving the army and I was carrying Andrew and trying to find somewhere to live.'

'That's hard, in someone else's house, with a young baby and another one on the way.'

'Lyd came. She was a great help. Then when Jack got a job, and we had our own house, it was easy having Pat and David.'

In Spring Woods the children raced ahead under the beeches. Pat was first to the Wishing Well, then Hatty with her golden hair, then Harry, dark and curly. David came last.

'Wish!' cried Hatty.

Each of them picked up a pebble and threw it into the well. The little pool was dark and cool within its stone enclosure built into the bank. The stone arch had a text. 'Ho, everyone that thirsteth, come ye to the waters, and he that hath no money.'

The well was full of stones. When his companions rushed away and forgot their wishes, David knelt down and scooped up water with cupped hands. He was about to drink when he heard Aunt Tilly behind him.

'I shouldn't do that, old lad. The kids all piddle in it.'

They followed the path along the edge of the wood in the fold of the valley. The path, overhung with beeches, skirted a corn field. The ears, ripening for harvest, whispered softly at the women's secrets.

'Pity Jack couldn't have seen his boys growing up,' Tilly said.

'I used to tell him the boys would look after us when we grew old. Jack said we would never grow old. He was like that. A boy who would never grow up. Peter Pan. In spite of all he went through in the war, he was always a little boy at heart.'

'Playing his mouth organ,' said Tilly. 'Do you remember his last leave, when we all went on the river with Lyd and the kids. That thunderstorm. It nearly drowned us, and we put you and the children on the towpath. Jack and I took the boat back, and we all met at the bridge, drenched to the skin. And Jack pulled out his mouth organ and marched us home.'

'It was all a big joke to him. Just a boy's prank. Getting wet through and singing to forget the trouble he would be in when he got home.'

'Men,' Tilly said dismissively. 'They're all a bit like kids. Especially soldiers, having to do what they're told. Everything found. All their clothes like school uniform. Getting up in the morning, going to meals, getting back at night and going to bed. Everything done by the bugle.'

'Keeping clean and tidy, and their boots polished,' laughed Nell. 'And another thing. Wanting to be heroes. Jack wanted to be a hero. He needn't have gone to France, you know, Tilly. He could have stayed in England and been a drill sergeant. Then, after all those years fighting, to lose his stripes like he did. Just because he let a German prisoner go to the lavatory. That's what he told me.'

'One little mistake. It makes you sick when you think of all the blunders those generals and politicians made before it all ended.'

'The strange thing was, he never felt any bitterness,' said Nell. 'He loved his regiment as much at the end as he did when he joined. I used to tell him he loved his regiment more than me. Do you know, Tilly, he never once had his photo taken out of uniform.'

Nell, strangely calm, seemed to be looking forward instead of back.

Forward to a reunion without soldiers and wars. She gazed at the children in the distance, jumping noisily up and down and quarrelling on the stile at the end of the footpath where it joined the road opposite the church.

'Shit socks,' Pat shouted at David, and wrestled with him until the women came.

'Let's go in the church,' Nell said.

Aunt Tilly's children had both been christened there. When Hatty was tiny she was taken to Sunday Matins. During the responses she shouted 'I don't like that song, mummy.' Tilly said 'You should have seen the faces when they turned round to look at the little hussy.' The old parson was ga-ga, always in a muddle, losing his place in the prayers, announcing wrong hymns and psalms, He trained theological students at the vicarage. Before they left the two women knelt and prayed and put coins in the box.

They stopped to watch a cricket match on the village green. The spectators included people with weekend cottages nearby – politicians and professionals, Bohemian stage people, authors, artists and musicians. Tilly knew them all. One of them was a lord. He had a towered mansion in the distance among the trees. The diaries of all these notables were known. Tilly got her information from village shopkeepers and tradesmen, gardeners, chauffeurs, domestics, who liked to have a gossip about what they knew.

The steep path down into the valley led them through the thicket where nightingales sang and bottle-tits nested. At the bottom, a chalk pit gaped at a patch of grass where gypsies had left the charred remains of their fires. They crossed the road and followed a path through more undergrowth. Golfers drove over the chalk and bocage to the Bulley Pit above the valley path. The children foraged for lost balls in the brambles. Pat found one and picked out yards of elastic. 'David's brains,' he said. 'He must have lost them. They've gone rotten.' He threw the rubbery ruin at his brother. 'Here you are, David,' he said. 'Have your brains back.' The brothers wrestled until the women came.

The Bulley Pit, a huge hole in the ground, the shape of a bucket, had a green at the bottom with a red metal flag. Golfers used wooden steps, but the children rolled down over the bumpy grass to the bottom. After each descent they climbed back to the top and rolled down again. When Nell and Tilly came they scolded them for getting dirty.

The valley path folded the Common into halves. They crossed it to the grassy slope the other side. Nell struggled breathlessly. David gave her an arm. Contrasting Nell's slight figure, Tilly, tall and wide-hipped, heavy on her enormous feet, climbed strongly, and her burnished hair glinted in the sun. Nell had no breath for words. She stopped to rest, and gazed across the valley to the gaping chalk. Tilly wandered to the right towards Cherry Links. Nell and David followed. They all sat down on the bank in the shade of the old cherry trees. The trees were riddled with woodpecker holes. The women relaxed on the sward and talked.

'Paradise,' Nell said. Beauty and peace surrounded them.

Pat and David performed handstands and cartwheels on the apron of green below the banks. Hatty and Harry imitated them.

'You'll be in trouble,' said Tilly. 'Here comes the greenkeeper.'

She nodded towards a little old man, bent and slow, struggling with wheelbarrow, clippers and broom.

'Old Father Time,' Tilly said.

Weary and dispirited, plagued by townee trippers and children, the old man strove to keep his fairways clear, his links undamaged, mown and green. Where dead wood cluttered, he cleared it away. Where growth defied him, he cut it down, and battled against brambles with bill hook and shears.

'Time to go,' Aunt Tilly said.

In the beech woods, trees lay felled. On the Common, arsenists had fired great patches of gorse into charred wastes.

'Vandals,' Tilly said. 'Why can't they let things grow.'

On their way home they passed the Sanatorium, hidden in trees. The children stared through the fence at patients covered with red blankets in beds and wheelchairs under the verandahs. They whispered to each other about the horrors of tuberculosis, and frightened themselves. The splashes of red warned them away, but they gaped and lingered. In this paradise there was a demon, a dark angel with a finger of death writing in blood on the wall.

'Hurry, children,' Tilly shouted. 'You'll miss the bus.'

They rushed to the safety and reassurance of their mothers.

At *Peacehaven* Tilly picked peas and soft fruit for Nell to take home. Then they all hurried to the bus. When it came they kissed and said goodbye.

'Good luck, Nell. Get well soon,' said Tilly.

'Thank-you again,' Nell said tearfully.

Chapter 8

To round off his first year at Sivier's, David, with Nell, deserted the Salvation Army and attended, with the Mayor and Corporation, the special end of term service at St. Edmund's. The church filled to overflowing. The bishop processed with mitre and crook, and preached the sermon. Senior scholars read the lessons. 'Let us now praise famous men and our fathers that begat us,' one of them began.

David had not known his father. He knew no famous men, only a drunk at home, a gambler next door, a drunken bully a few doors away, and the Band of Hope man who played with his privates. He praised his mother. Her righteousness would never be forgotten. 'Charity suffereth long and is kind,' the next boy read, and when he had finished, David understood that his mother, a queen, as great as any woman could be, knew as much about Charity as St. Paul. He followed her in the pointing of the Psalm, No. 15, the gentleman's psalm, confident that no gentleman could be as good as her, and that she would be at home with the Lord in his house on the Holy Hill.

The following week Nell went into hospital. Pat went to camp, David to Isleworth, and they met again at *Peacehaven*, Aunt Tilly's cottage in the Chilterns, choc-a-bloc with children.

Born a Londoner, Aunt Tilly had deserted the city and left behind a widowed mother and two brothers and their families. Every Easter the families came to *Peacehaven*. The wives told Tilly how beautiful it all was, and how the kids loved it, and how lucky to live in the country where you could turn them out without worrying. Not like Deptford where the kids were always in trouble in school holidays. Tilly would spread her arms aloft and say 'Let them come here.'

Without gas or electricity, and only a tap in the scullery sink, the cottage was ill equipped for visitors. For cooking there was only the kitchen fire with a small oven at the side.

'Fetch some sticks,' Tilly shouted. 'Fill up the kettles and saucepans.' She pressed a handful of kindling on the glowing embers. Every meal began with a blaze.

Nicknamed 'Chief' for being head of the tribe, Tilly had the biggest of the three bedrooms, but never seemd to be more than half married. Mondays to Thursdays, alone and sleepless, she spent the nights reading and solving crossword puzzles by oil lamp. From the County library she borrowed a stack of romantic novels, mystery thrillers and biographies. They were her substitute for sleep. In the morning, fresh as a daisy, she rose before anyone else, stirred the ashes, rekindled the fire and boiled the kettle for the first tea.

Her two children shared the middle bedroom. The rest crowded into the third and overflowed onto the landing and into the sitting room downstairs where they slept on easy chairs, or on the floor, or wherever they could. In the inevitable quarrels, Pat and David established a cameraderie they had not known before, and took themselves off with a billycan picnic, marched into the hills, picked blackberries for Aunt Tilly, and came back kippered from camp fires. Wet days, everyone stayed indoors. High spirited and noisy, the children trod the chairs. 'That's enough of that,' ruled Aunt Tilly, and found board games and jig-saws for them to play with. For Pat and David she pulled out a pile of old war magazines gathering dust in the cupboard. They browsed through them and searched in vain for a picture of their father in the trenches.

Gran, bulging under the strings of her apron, took charge in Cheese Row. Her yellow, drooping face proclaimed that life was draining away. Wilmot had gone. The uncles had turned him out.

'When's mum coming home?' David asked George, but got no answer. 'When are you going to see her?' he persisted.

'Saturday. That's next visiting day. Saturday afternoon.'

'I'll come with you,' David said.

'That'll be alright. She wants to see you. We'll all go and take some flowers.'

Gran cast a shadow. 'You won't be able to see her,' she said. 'They don't allow more than two. Your aunt and uncle will be there.'

'So we're going to see them at last,' Pat said.

Gran pounced. 'That's enough from you,' she said. 'Just you show a bit of respect.' She waddled round and complained of the chores. 'Never thought I'd be doing this again. Looking after kids.'

'We're not kids,' said Pat. 'Kids are goats. They've got horns.'

'The devil's got horns, and you're a little devil,' Gran said, and leaned on the bare, scrubbed table, and waved Pat away. 'Get out of here before I give you a hiding!' she yelled.

Saturday afternoon George and Andrew with a bunch of yellow and bronze chrysanthemums rode their bikes to the hospital. Pat and David took the tram.

The building, cube on cube of Bath stone, towered over Pat and David. They felt lost in the huge gravel forecourt. The entrance, between tall, fluted columns, could have led into the Judgement Hall at the end of the world. The boys approached with nervous hesitation, but gained confidence as they merged with other visitors ascending the wide, stone steps from the forecourt. The porter at this palace of pain and death, in navy blue uniform, told them where to go, but they were soon lost in a maze of green painted corridors. A nurse rescued them and took them to Adelaide Ward.

Uncle Dick and Aunt Annie were waiting to go in. They lived in Potters Row, around the corner from Cheese Row, but the boys did not know them very well. Nell's youngest brother Dick had been a professional footballer until a knee injury finished his career. David and his brothers used to boast about him to their mates. Now they had a chance to study him at close quarters. He did not look so bad, built like an athlete, very fair, rather solemn, like Gran. Aunt Annie, tall, erect, dark and beautiful, held a brown paper bag of fruit.

'Hulloh, boys,' they said, smiled, and lapsed into silence.

The two boys walked down the corridor to ease the tension, and leaned against the wall. Impatiently, they came back to their aunt and uncle.

'We've got to wait a bit,' said Uncle Dick. 'Your brothers are in there.' From his waistcoat pocket he withdrew a gold watch on the end of a chain and glanced at it anxiously.

Pat and David nodded their understanding.

When George and Andrew came out, Uncle Dick explained that he and Aunt Annie were in a hurry, so they would go in next.

'I bet they're going to Elm Park. It's a Derby game. Reading and Swindon.' said Pat.

'Mum wants to see the four of us together,' George said.

'Gran said we couldn't,' Pat said.

'Mum asked the sister. She's letting us all go in at the end.'

'When is she coming home?' asked Pat, but got no reply.

'Has she still got that lump on her throat?' David asked.

'Yes,' said George.

'Do her hands still shake?'

George, reluctant to answer, left it to Andrew.

'You'll see,' Andrew said.

The uncle and aunt did not keep them waiting long. Nell welcomed her boys with hugs and kisses. David gave her half-a-dozen eggs. Pat had wanted to bring them, but Gran said they would be safer with David. They were the last from Wilmot's hens.

'Lovely,' said Nell. 'Just what I wanted.'

David put them away in her locker.

Nell's bed was on the short, inside wall of the ward. Sunlight streamed through the high windows. Smells tainted the air. The faces of other patients showed between the dark clothes of their visitors.

David looked closely at his mother. She seemed no better than before. 'And how are my two schoolboys?' she asked.

'Alright, mum,' they said together.

'Are you being a good boy, Pat?'

She asked the question more in the nature of a joke than a serious enquiry, and posed it smilingly, as though she knew the answer, but it did not matter, as long as he was at her side, safe and sound, fed and cared for. Clean and smart in school uniform, Pat grinned and wriggled shyly, ill at ease in the strange, sterile surroundings.

'He's alright,' George said. 'No trouble.'

Pat gave his mother an account of the boys' camp at Hastings. David brought messages of love from Jack's folk at Isleworth. The two boys entertained Nell with stories of their adventures with Aunt Tilly.

When Nell had quizzed them long enough for her to know what was going on in the world, she pointed to the grand piano in the middle of the ward between the patients beds. On top of it, vases of flowers were soaking up the sun.

'Isn't it a beauty?' Nell said. 'Sister says Andrew can come one evening and play. And David can sing.'

A nurse rang a hand bell.

'Time to go,' Nell said sadly, as though it was her that was leaving them.

The boys kissed her goodbye, and waved from the door before they left.

On a dark, autumnal, October evening, Andrew and David, washed and brushed in Sunday best, set out to entertain the patients of Adelaide Ward to a musical evening. David, perched on the cross bars of Andrew's bike, clutched a bundle of music against the handlebars. It was uphill all the way against the wind. David sat uncomfortably on the hard, cold steel. Andrew struggled to Northgate, skirted the Abbey to Eastgate, crossed the Orts Bridge and climbed the hill into the London Road. The high windows of the hospital glared with electrics.

The sister took them under her wing and opened the piano. Nervously, Andrew made himself comfortable on the circular, revolving stool. He opened his music and started straight in with *Maiden's Prayer*. After that he played Mendelsshon's *Chanson Triste*. Then David sang Gounod's *Nazareth* and followed with the concert setting of *Abide With Me*. Andrew played a *Chanson Sans Paroles*, then a Chopin *Nocturne*, and finished with a Brahms *Cradle Song*.

The patients applauded. 'Nice,' said some. 'Lovely,' said others. Nell, propped with pillows, looked proudly on, choked with emotion.

Sister closed the piano and put back the flowers. The boys collected their music and walked over to their mother. She could find no words, but kissed them both and damped their faces with her tears. Doctors and nurses beamed at the young performers, then got on with their work. Sister gave them tea and cakes, molly-coddled them, kidded them along and asked them to come again.

'Kiss me again,' Nell sobbed, her pleasure mixed with sadness at the conviction of her own departure. The boys lingered at the door and waved.

Outside, in the cold, damp night, the brothers found the bike lying on the ground, struck down by the wind. Andrew picked it up, turned the pedal and heard it scrape the frame. Unable to straighten the crank, he pushed the bicycle home. David walked alongside with the music. In a sad and silent drop from heights, they descended from the euphoria of the hospital on the hill to the depression of their house in the valley.

Each summer, as each life, is unique, and writes its epitaph in the sapless leaves. How transient, autumn's melancholy touch. Ribs and rings of morning dew disappear in the twinkling of an eye. Mists gather on the river and disperse. Fruit falls into a pool. The water rings expand into nothing.

Nell weakened with the autumn sun until she died. On a rough, drenching day full of spite, a damp paste sky blocked the eye of the sun. Leaves scrambled along wet pavements, spun to and fro like lost children. In the vast vacancy of the hospital forecourt the aunts and uncles assembled to ask themselves the old questions. Nell was dying. Would she gain freedom, or suffer imprisonment in the grave? Death. Is it joy or sorrow? Hope or horror? They pushed David into the centre of their uncertainty. Nell wanted to see him, but they were loath to grant her wish. They had no precedents, no guide lines. The problems unsettled them. How would the death bed affect one so young, they asked themselves, and judged the boy too green to be acquainted with death.

'Your mother wants to see you,' said Uncle Hugh, the eldest, a big man.

David had not thought of his mother dying, so he was ready, and waited for a hand to take him to her. Instead, they crowded and encircled him, as though for protection.

'It might upset you,' said Uncle Dick.

'You don't have to go,' said Aunt Annie.

He wanted to go, but these solemn relations were offering an easy option they preferred him to take. He had to make a decision where none was necessary. One of them should have stepped forward, clasped his shoulder, spoken words of comfort, led him to his mother. He felt the weight of their concern and lacked the will to oppose them, step out of the circle and go his way alone.

Nell died in the night. David dug a hole to bury his guilt, and found a spectre.

Black horses led the cortége at a trot, tapped out a dance macabre, drummed the mourners to the Citadel. The captain said that Nell might have asked God why he had forsaken her. Instead, she made herself a sacrifice for him for a sweet smelling savour, because in secret she had sanctified her fast. In honour, patience, purity, long-suffering and kindness, she had borne her afflictions and labours. Angels had ministered to her and brought her to this day of salvation. Faithful unto death, she had run the race and would receive the prize of eternal inheritance. Her treasure was in heaven. Her sons, born of the freewoman, children of promise, should listen to the word of God and keep it. He that is not with God is against him. A house divided against itself will fall.

Lidded down under the wreaths, she was laid in a quiet corner by the last post of the cemetery, with no cover but earth, no marble edge, no urn, no lapidary headstone, no sculptured image to mock her memory. An image should not be attempted, any more for Nell than for God himself. Who can paint a paradox, a holy mystery? What picture could comprehend her maiden bloom, the milk of her breast, the gigantism of the goitre, the comfort of her trembling hand?

Her children were blown like leaves, sapless, severed from the capillaries of root, stem and stalk. Friends and neighbours stared and saw them in heroic terms, facing tasks, and handicapped, the odds against them. Aunt Tilly went to the Citadel, but was not invited to the breakfast. No one came from Isleworth.

When tears were neatly dried, Gran passed round the food. 'Don't be greedy,' she warned Pat.

The aunts chattered.

'The flowers were lovely.'

'A real picture.'

'Nell would have enjoyed them.'

'A pity they die so soon.'

'What a price they are.'

Uncle Dick produced a silver flask and handed it round. 'Have a swig. Warm the cockles of your heart.'

'Thanks, Dick. I was ready for that.'

'Cheers! A drop of good stuff.'

The flask came back to Uncle Dick. 'Here's to poor Nell,' he said, and took a sip. 'That's better. I needed that.' He wiped the mouth of the flask, screwed on the cap, and returned it to his hip pocket.

Aunt Annie produced a bottle of sherry, 'I don't see why the men should be the only ones to have a bit of comfort,' she said, and poured some for the women. They drank to Nell's memory.

The men smoked.

When the food had gone the aunts and uncles formed a planning committee to decide the future and divide up the house. The boys were sent into the front room.

'I think I'm going to live with Uncle Hugh,' George said.

'I'm going to Uncle Dick's,' Andrew said.

'I'm going to Chorley Wood to Aunt Rose,' Pat said. 'I don't want to go.'

'You'll be alright,' George said. 'It's nice there.'

'It's nice here,' Pat said. 'All my mates are here. I shan't know anyone.'

'You'll soon find plenty of mates,' Andrew said.

'Where am I going?' David asked.

'That's what they're talking about in there,' George said.

It was out of their hands. Minors, with no power of veto, they had to do as they were told. It had all happened so suddenly, like an earthquake, everything ruined. Each boy, still suffering from shock, felt weak, hardly conscious of what was going on around them. Before the funeral Gran disposed of the rubbish – old papers, cleaning rags, disused clothes, broken things – and burnt them in the scullery copper. Some items had been disputed. George saved some old letters, postcards and photos from the fire. Pat argued with Gran about his crystal set. She said it was junk. His aunt would have no room for it. Pat raised the roof. 'You old witch,' he said, and got a backhander as he struggled with her, but failed to snatch the cat's whisker from the flames. Afterwards he cried.

Much of the furniture and things in the kitchen and bedrooms had no value. Nell had never carried much surplus. Her best things in the front room, which she treasured and polished, went to her younger sister who, soon afterwards, married and took over the house. Nell's silver locket with Jack's photo, which she wore on a black cord round her neck, went to George. He also got her wedding ring.

While the four boys were alone together in the front room they shared out the contents of the mahogany box from the corner cupboard. Each of them had a medal with its ribbon. David got the Mons Star, dull and tinny looking, the crown above the star tarnished, the colours of the silk ribbon watered into each other, as though it had been wet with tears. Each boy got a bent bullet and a few photos. David got a French brooch and blue bead necklace. The division made without dispute, they took their mementoes upstairs and put them in their bags packed ready for departure.

Uncle Dick and Aunt Annie told David they wanted to talk to him on his own in the front room.

'You've been a bit of a problem,' Uncle Dick said solemnly, then grinned to indicate he was joking.

'We've been fighting over you,' Aunt Annie said, and smiled, as though sharing the joke with her husband.

'We all wanted you,' said Uncle Dick.

'You're the favourite,' said Aunt Annie.

'We can't upset your schooling,' said Uncle Dick. 'George is going to Uncle Hugh and Andrew is coming to us. Uncle Albert hasn't any room. That's why Pat is going to Chorley Wood. That leaves you.'

'Later on, you'll be going to board at Sivier's,' said Aunt Annie. 'Until then we thought the best thing would be for you to come to us for six months, then go to Uncle Hugh until you start boarding at the school in September.'

'Will that be alright?' asked Uncle Dick.

They had been one family, one body. Now, anaesthetised on the operating table, the body was being dismembered. The grown-ups had worked it all out for the best. David nodded approval.

The brothers fetched their bags and went their different ways.

Chapter 9

To withstand the assaults of oncoming winter a young scion needs the nourishment and support of a binding affinity with its host. A sapling transplanted to new surroundings should be firmly bedded and supported. Wing footed Perseus with his pruning sickle leaves a trail of dead sticks in the equinoctial gales, bringing death to what is weak on the tree and loose in the ground.

From the house in Cheese Row which faced south, Andrew and David moved round the corner to a house in Potters Row which faced north. To David, the rooms seemed dark and strange. Andrew, persuaded to uproot himself from engineering, became a metal sorter at the rag and bone yard where Uncle Dick was foreman. Aunt Annie wanted Andrew to be happy. She said 'How miserable not to be allowed to go to the pictures, or have a smoke and a drink with your uncle.' So he gave up the Salvation Army and became a great favourite with his aunt. She would do anything for him. They discovered they liked the same film stars. She spent a lot of her afternoons at the movies – four times a week when the features changed on Thursday.

Aunt Annie, a dark, Romany beauty, came from a gypsy family which had given up its precarious existence, burnt its caravans and moved into numbered houses in named streets. No great homelover, housekeeper or cook, she favoured bead curtains and artificial flowers. For going out she dressed in black with a red fox stole, black silk stockings and high heels. She suffered a weak heart. When she had what she called a 'turn' she stood holding the mantelpiece and sipped brandy. Uncle Dick rubbed her

84

back until the wind came up and she felt better.

Uncle Dick, fair haired and blue eyed, not very tall, still looked athletic. War had interrupted his football career. On discharge from the army he signed professional and, for a few seasons, earned good money. Then he tore a cartilage and never played again. In his hey-day, he and Aunt Annie spent what he earned and lived it up. There was a little compensation, but it did not last long, and he went back to his old job at the rag and bone yard. He suffered a fall. Life had not fulfilled its promise. His dream had ended.

Esther, a pretty little red-head, was their only child. She had a small, pale face. When she smiled she showed her tiny, yellow teeth, defective from too many toffees and sweets and not enough brush. She welcomed David as an elder brother. 'Have you seen my dad's caps and medals?' she asked, knowing how much he liked playing football, and took him into the front room and opened the corner cupboard. The trophies lay in a neglected heap. Esther shook the dust off one of the tasselled schoolboy international caps and put it on David's head. Then she pinned a medal on his shirt and boosted his pride.

It was the only encouragement he got. David expected his uncle to treat him like a son and teach him some football skills, but, because of his own bitter experience, Uncle Dick chose not to encourage his nephew's ambitions in a game which had let him down. 'Help him get ready,' Aunt Annie urged her husband when David was preparing for a house game. Uncle Dick laid down his newspaper and embrocated the boy's legs.

The smell put David off. He learnt more about playing cards than football. In the evenings, midweek, his aunt and uncle stayed home and played cribbage, a few pence a game, and drank bottled beer, cheap light dinner ale for him, milk stout for her. Sometimes Andrew joined them. The rhythm of the scoring danced in David's brain. 'Fifteen-two, fifteen-four, fifteen-six, a pair eight, and one for his nob, nine.'

Dick Tulloch and his wife had no religion. Weekends they socialised at their favourite pubs. Dick's friend who lived near the ice factory had a sister who baby-minded Esther and David when the grown-ups went out in the evening. She was a shorthand typist, wore spectacles with thick lenses, and had a carnose attractiveness. She and the two children played simple card and board games. Under the noisy gaslight the cards would be spread for clock patience on the green baize table cloth. Suddenly the baby-minder would burst into tears, and she would dive into her handbag for a handkerchief, take off her glasses, dry her eyes and blow her nose. 'He's let me down again, the brute. I don't know why I bother with him,' she would say. Her romantic relationship was with one of Aunt Annie's brothers, but he was a tearaway and made dates with her and did not bother to turn up. 'Come and sit on my lap,' she would say to David.

Missing the close, physical relationship with his mother, the boy welcomed the attentions of the fubsy young woman. For consolation, she cuddled him in a bosomy rapture. The boy needed Nell's sweet smelling savour. Instead, the baby-minder sweated under the oxters and repelled him.

Nothing went right. The Tullochs and their extended family went to a Christmas party at the friend's house near the ice factory. David the scholarship boy, expected to shine in the memory games, the puzzles and riddles requiring brains, was nervous amongst all the strangers. Over-anxious to please, he succumbed to the pressure and failed. He suffered the isolation of lost status and feared his aunt and uncle would not love him any more. On that cold, snow-deep Christmas they were silent as they marched him home through the icy, slippery, hostile streets. Esther did not mind. She was dumb too, and held his hand.

Esther lost David to Trixie, and he exchanged life in Potters Row for Workhouse Lane, another terrace. The house had the distinction of a bay window and a porch entrance. It had an aura of well-being.

Uncle Hugh looked down on his family out of a framed enlargement of a photograph showing him in army breeches and shirt sleeves on some Eastern Mediterranean shore. He had carried his army smartness into civilian life. As a bus driver in the local Transport Department he wore a peaked hat, a red corded, metal buttoned, navy blue serge tunic with shoulder straps, navy blue serge breeches with fornicator flap, and black leather gaiters. He went to work with a spit and polish spruceness. Everyone said he was the best driver on the corporation buses and would soon be an Inspector.

Aunt Emmy, small and wiry, reminded David of his mother, the way she cooked, and worked in the house. For going out with her husband, her neat, well cut, home-made clothes were made smart by a silver fox stole, rivalling Aunt Annie's, whose fox was red.

Colin, their eldest, a printer like George, was a year or two older. Pam, about George's age, was blonde, pretty, vivacious, dance crazy, worked on the millinery counter of a town centre store, and made all her own frocks. Trixie, the youngest of the cousins, about David's age, was blonde, plump, dimple pretty and boisterous.

George had already lived there six months and had put down roots. He and David made the house crowded. They shared the small back bedroom with Colin, who should have had it for himself. Nevertheless, Colin, a fair haired giant, big framed like his father, welcomed David as a younger brother. George was too old for him to have fun with, but he took liberties with David, tossed him about and tickled him on the bed. 'Come here, you young cub,' he would say, and grab the youngster, and tickle him until he was screaming for Colin to stop. David had never experienced such horseplay from his older brothers. Colin laughed and let the lad go, but the protests inhibited their behaviour, and, when the jostling stopped, David blamed himself for being a spoilsport and decided Colin did not love him any more.

There was a piano in the front room. Colin, at the age when a boy needs to thump something, thumped the piano – jazz tunes. George, learning the saxaphone for the Salvation Army band, accompanied him. Pam and her friends joined in the song and dance. There was no room for Trixie and David in this adolescent sport, so, when Uncle Hugh and Aunt Emmy were out, they were left to themselves in the back kitchen. Trixie's friend Belle came in and they had fun in the dark. Tight as buds, without consciousness of sin, the children excited each other as male and female, normal and uncomplicated.

David and Trixie were wrestling in the front garden.

'Do you like Belle?' Trixie asked.

'She's alright,' David said.

'She likes boys,' said Trixie.

'So do you, don't you?'

'Not like Belle. She's naughty. She takes her clothes off.'

'Why does she do that?'

'Boys like it, don't they?'

They giggled. At the side of the dirt path where the washing hung, a low rail protected the spring flowers. Rose buds were forming on the trellis behind the outside loo. Trixie's hair fell over her smooth, round shoulders. Her face was pretty and dimpled. 'She fancies you,' she said. 'We're going out this afternoon. She wants you to come.'

'Where are you going?'

'Westbrook.'

It was the place to go with the girls. The back road led under the railway arch and turned into a dirt track all the way to the Thames. Ditches separated the track from the allotments, beyond which there was just waste land with a lot of bushes.

David was tempted, but had arranged to play cricket in the park; just kid's stuff with an old bat and ball, a few odd wickets, and four boys, enough for a batsman, a bowler, a longstop and someone to run for the ball in the outfield. Cricket meant more to him than Belle. He turned Trixie down and told her why.

'Silly old cricket,' Trixie said, and ran indoors in a huff.

In the evening, before leaving Trixie and David alone in the house, Aunt Emmy told them not to be too late going to bed.

David had not been able to talk to Trixie since coming back from his afternoon in the park. When they were alone he made a fresh start. 'How did you get on this afternoon?' he asked. 'Tell me all about it.'

'There's nothing to tell.'

'Did Belle find someone else?'

'No one likes her. She's too fast.'

'Why do you go with her?'

'She's alright sometimes, but I wouldn't do what she does.'

'You're much too nice.'

Trixie smiled at last and showed her dimples. 'And you're too nice for Belle,' she said.

'What happened, then?'

'She took the boy I went with. They went off into the bushes and left me to come home on my own.'

'I'm sorry,' David said.

'No you're not. If you'd been there instead of playing your rotten old cricket we could have had fun.'

They sat on opposite sides of the table under the gaslight. Trixie tossed away her hair and looked arch. 'She's coming round tonight. She'll be here soon.'

Dark eyed, dark haired Belle arrived and the two girls quarrelled. Trixie decided to have an early night. She got herself some supper and went to bed.

Belle stayed on and cut herself a slice of bread. 'I love bread and butter,' she said, and, spreading the butter thickly, greased her long, plump shapely fingers and sucked them. While eating she drew close to

David, put her arm round his neck and stroked his face. She had beautiful, midnight blue eyes, but the smell of her hands was sickening.

'Who did you go with this afternoon?' David asked.

'No one you know. He's silly and slow. I like you much better.'

Her breath smelled greasy too. David got a whiff of it when she kissed him. Belle was guiding David's hands into her secret places when Trixie came down for a book and interrupted them.

'Don't forget what mummy said about not being too late going to bed,' Trixie said, and went upstairs.

Belle cut herself another slice of bread, piled on the butter, licked her fingers and started to eat. 'Kiss me,' she said with her mouth full.

'I ought to be going to bed,' David said. Belle gave him a sensation in the nerve ends, a stirring in the derm, a movement he had not known before, but the smell of her breath and her hands nauseated and repelled him.

'Take me with you,' Belle said. 'Let's have fun.'

Neither were ready for that. She spoke out of devilment, not meaning what she said. David got up and prepared some supper for himself.

'Aren't you going to kiss me?' Belle asked.

'I'm going to bed,' David said.

'You're slow,' Belle said. 'And silly, like that boy this afternoon.' She stood up and licked her fingers. 'Thanks for nothing,' she said, and walked out and slammed the doors.

David ate his supper and went upstairs. As he passed through the middle bedroom he said goodnight to Trixie. He got into bed, but could not sleep, and was still awake when the grown-ups came back.

May Day, which should have been a dance, was a General Strike. The men at Workhouse Lane stayed home all week, but by Saturday needed to get out of the house to relieve the general gloom. Uncle Hugh and Aunt Emmy met friends at the Labour Club. Colin took his girl to see Reginald Denny in *California Straight Ahead* – with 3000 miles of laughter on the way. Pam and her boyfriend went dancing at Olympia. George attended a Salvation Army wedding at the Citadel. And while they were all out, Trixie and David sat cheek to cheek and laughed at Charley Chaplin in *Funny Wonder*.

Aunt Emmy had a secret complaint that no one talked about. On Sunday morning, while she slept late, Uncle Hugh organised the weekly chores. Everyone had a job. Colin cleaned the cutlery, Pam prepared lunch, George swept floors, Trixie did the dusting, and David helped his uncle polish the furniture.

Colin switched on the AJS three valve cabinet radio to get the news. 'Things will never be the same again,' his father said.

The sun streamed through the living room window. Uncle Hugh dabbed a cloth on the open tin of Mansion Polish and rubbed it on the wireless cabinet.

'Will we win?' Colin asked, and brandished the carver.

'Of course,' said his father, 'We've got to.'

Trixie whispered in David's ear and made him giggle. They giggled together and relieved the solemnity and tension.

'I'm not so sure,' said Colin. His face was strong and angular. A thick brush of hair hung over his forehead. His shirt was unbuttoned at the neck, the sleeves rolled to the elbows. He held the carver with two hands, one at the point of the blade, the other on the handle. 'What about all them volunteers running the buses and trams?' he asked.

'And all the special constables,' said George, holding a dust pan and brush. 'There's a lot of people against us.'

Uncle Hugh turned a chair upside down and polished the legs. 'Don't believe all you hear on the news,' he said.

Pam shouted from the scullery. 'Dad, d'you know what I saw on a poster? It said, don't listen to the wireless, come along to Whitley Pump and hear the truth.'

Aunt Emmy appeared, looking pale, and joined in the laughter. She said she had seen a food lorry making deliveries. It had GRUB chalked on the side.

Trixie chimed in to say she had seen a milk cart chalked with 'Mother, here's the juice.'

'Trixie, really!' Pam scolded, but laughed with her mother and the men. Trixie laughed and showed her dimples.

'Some of the buses are running,' Colin said.

'Blacklegs,' said George.

'Scabs,' said Colin.

'You're right,' said Uncle Hugh. 'We've got some of them in the trams.' He bent over to polish the table. David followed with a shining rag. The sun complimented their work.

Colin put the carver away and took out another knife from the drawer of the dresser. He said 'They reckon six men were arrested the other night when they tried to stop a tram getting back to the depot.'

'It takes guts to fight the police,' said Uncle Hugh. 'Martyrs. That's what they are. Martyrs.'

'Fighting for their principles,' said George. 'That's all they were doing. Fighting for what's right.'

Pam, drying her hands on her apron, came in from the scullery. She looked pretty in a clean, blue apron, and showed off her pretty legs and the Saturday night wave in her hair. 'I had to laugh the other morning,' she said. 'Just along from the store where the tram stops there was a crowd of people fighting, trying to stop the tram. Then someone from an upstairs window poured a bucket of water over them. Laugh? I nearly died.'

Uncle Hugh looked serious. A coachbuilder at the Transport Depot had been ordered by an official of the National Union of Vehicle Workers to stop work or he would be thrown in the river, and his wife would be given hell, if they did not leave the town and work somewhere else. The blackleg was taking the union man to court.

Colin and George were silent. The story made the issues more complex. They needed time to think about it. When was a martyr not a martyr?

'Just shows how careful you have to be,' Uncle Hugh said.

'What about this meeting at the Labour Club tonight?' asked Colin. 'You're speaking, aren't you?'

'They've asked me to,' said Uncle Hugh.

'I'd love to hear you,' said Pam.

'There could be trouble,' said Aunt Emmy. 'Fighting.'

'Sounds exciting,' said Trixie. 'Can I go?'

'No, my girl,' said Aunt Emmy. 'It will be past your bedtime. And I don't think Pam should go either, unless Colin or George goes with her.'

'I've got a date,' Colin said.

'I'm going,' George said. 'You can come with me Pam.'

Pam had plenty of escorts, but George would do. She had other things on her mind beside the General Strike. 'I bought some dress material yesterday,' she said, and waited for her mother's response.

'Well, aren't you going to let me see it?' Aunt Emmy said.

'I'll fetch it,' said Pam, and ran upstairs. She came down carrying a large brown paper parcel with a hat on top.

Aunt Emmy picked up the hat. 'It's lovely,' she said.

'Do you like it?'

Pam took the hat, held it at arm's length and studied it. The creation, covered with crepe-de-chine with an under-brim of straw to match, had a crown swathed in multi-coloured material, and a scarf. Pam put it on and bent her head this way and that in front of the mirror over the mantelpiece. She patted and pressed her hair to suit the tilt of the hat.

'It's nice. It suits you,' Aunt Emmy said.

Pam kept the hat on while she showed her mother the contents of the parcel. She described the items; a length of silk and cotton Marocain in a soft shade of pink; a gaberdine wrap coat trimmed with braid and fastened by a single button; a pair of shoes in tan glacé with a lizard girdle. She had bought them specially for the visit of the Prince of Wales.

'My word, you have been splashing out,' said Aunt Emmy.

'Well, it's spring, isn't it?' Pam put on the new shoes and coat and looked at herself in the mirror.

'Pity the Prince isn't coming,' Trixie said mischievously. 'He would have fancied you in that.'

'Trixie,' scolded Aunt Emmy.

'Don't be cheeky,' said Pam.

Colin picked up the pink Marocain and draped it over himself. 'Anyone fancy me?' he asked. 'P'raps I'll get a new pair of Oxford bags to match.'

Pam undraped her brother and asked him when his girl was coming round because she wanted her help with the dressmaking.

David, fascinated by these strange new family relationships, watched dreamily, open-mouthed.

'Come on, young lad,' Uncle Hugh broke into his reverie. 'It's time you were off to church.'

Diana had gone. He had lost interest in the Salvation Army and joined the choir at St. Edmund's. The music teacher at Sivier's had persuaded him. Reluctantly, he left the fun, colour and femininity of his new adoptive family and prepared himself for church. George put on his Salvation Army uniform and picked up his flugal horn in its little black case. The two brothers left together.

Life had changed. After the matriarchy of Cheese Row, David was having to adapt to the patriarchy of his new surroundings. It was man, not woman, who ran things. At church it was the King the parson prayed for, and judges and policemen put in authority to minister justice and punish wickedness and vice. In the middle of prayer for the Church Militant the parson paused for the congregation to think about the National Disaster. All David could think about was Trixie, Pam and

Aunt Emmy, and how disappointed they were that the Prince had cancelled his visit to celebrate the centenary of the biscuit factory and open the new bridge across the Thames.

By Wednesday the strike was over. The men from Workhouse Lane went to the Labour Club and sang *The Red Flag*. They demanded that the new bridge be called 'Liberty Bridge'. With their comrades, and a police escort and a brass band, they marched over it to a mass meeting on the Recreation Ground. Mr. Baldwin, the Prime Minister, urged everyone to forget all bitterness, but the local MP rejoiced in the collapse of the revolutionary movement. The women at Workhouse Lane had a good laugh. 'Oh, these men,' they said to themselves.

Pam danced the Charleston to one of her Edison Bell Velvet Face records. David watched her. How pretty she was, the way she flapped her skirts up and down her shapely legs. She used to talk to her mother about Colin. 'He whisks his girl around as though she was a frockful of air. All the girls worship him. He could have anyone he wanted.' By Saturday after the strike, Pam had made her new dress, and all the young people went dancing to the music of The Melody Dance Orchestra at Olympia in London Street.

It was the year Percy Chapman, the local hero, was chosen to play for England against the Australians. Every day of the summer holidays David took sandwiches and played cricket in the public park. The boys pretended to be Maurice Tate, Percy Chapman, Jack Hobbs, or anyone they fancied, played six-day Tests from Monday to Saturday and compiled huge scores.

One day they had a spectator. A man parked his bicycle against the nearest elm. At the luncheon interval he made himself friendly and offered custard creams out of his food tin.

'I'm on holiday,' the man said, and smiled, drawing attention to his teeth, which looked too big for his mouth, and his full smooth lips, which looked like red rubber inner-tubes. 'I always spend my holidays at home. Never go away. Don't much like the sea. I go cycling on my tourer.'

The man nodded with his flat tweed cap towards his bicycle. The machine, with dropped handlebars covered with corrugated rubber material, looked strong and dependable, like the man himself in his tweedy jacket and knickerbockers, woollen stockings and heavy brown brogues. 'Have you all got bikes?' he asked, and stretched his thick, muscular legs on the grass.

They all had bikes except David. 'I haven't got one,' he said.

'Ask your dad to buy you one,' said the stranger.

'I haven't got a dad.'

'That's a shame. What happened to him?'

'Killed in the war.'

'You poor boy. What about your mother?'

'She's dead too.'

'You're an orphan, then. Who looks after you?'

'My aunt and uncle.'

'Well, David. That's your name isn't it? Do you mind if I call you David?'

'No. I don't mind.'

'If you haven't got a bike, how would you like to come riding with me one day?'

David liked the idea, and felt pleased that a man was taking a real interest and wanting to give him a treat.

'I like cricket,' said the stranger. 'I've never played, though. I used to keep the score once, but the club gave me the sack. They said I wasn't doing it right, but I didn't agree with them. D'you know, boys, that in the old days they kept the score by making notches on a stick?'

None of the boys knew that. It was interesting. An interesting man, David thought. Having eaten, they were eager to get on with the game.

'You don't mind if I stay and watch, do you boys?' the man asked.

Why should they mind. Having someone to watch was like playing at the Oval. They wore themselves out trying to impress their spectator. After all, he might be a scout – someone in disguise looking for young talent, like league clubs had for football. Their imaginations ran riot. At close of play they made arrangements for next day.

David, the only one without a bike, was left alone with the stranger. The two of them made their way to the park exit. The man pushed his bike with one hand and put his free arm round David's shoulder.

'You know, David, I've been watching you this afternoon. You're a nice lad. Much better than the others. They're a bit cocky, aren't they? Noisy. Now you, you're a quiet little chap. Intelligent, I'd say. Brainy. I like you, and I meant what I said about taking you for a ride in the country.'

David felt pleased with the compliments and the invitation.

'You don't get many treats, do you?' the man said, and David agreed.

Neither of his uncles had ever taken him anywhere.

'How long is it since your mother died?'

'Last October.'

'So you haven't lived with your aunt and uncle very long. How do you get on with them?'

'This is my second uncle. Before that I lived with another one.'

'Aunts and uncles are a funny lot. Very often they mean well, but sometimes it's difficult for a boy like you to talk to them, and they're not very interested anyway. Do your aunt and uncle ever want to know what you've been up to during the day? If I took you for a swim, for instance, would you have to tell them?'

'My aunt isn't very well. My uncle's a driver on the buses. I don't see him much. If I wanted a bathe I'd just go.'

'As a matter of fact, I thought of going for a swim tomorrow. Can you swim?'

David could swim. He had won two certificates at junior school.

'Well done,' the man said. 'Would you like to come swimming with me tomorrow?'

'Yes please,' David said.

'That's settled then. You play cricket in the morning. I'll be there about lunchtime. We'll go swimming in the afternoon. How's that?'

'That'll be alright,' David said.

'We'll go to Drowned Meadow. Do you know it? It's the other side of Pigney Bridge.'

David had heard of it, but never been. It would be interesting to see what it was like.

'Where do you live?' the man asked at the park exit.

'Workhouse Lane.'

'I know. Jump on. I'll give you a lift.'

The stranger mounted his bike and told David to hop on the step at the back and hold him tight round the waist. From the heights of the park, which separated the two river valleys, they speeded downhill towards the Thames, slowing and turning right into the busy Oxford Road.

At the house in Workhouse Lane, dance music floated over the waves into the living room. The family were about to have tea. Colin, Pam and George were humming, singing, tapping out the rhythms of the music. Aunt Emmy called Trixie from upstairs. Uncle Hugh put aside his newspaper, and they all sat down to eat. They told each other of the events of the day.

David felt isolated. Colin and Trixie had cooled. Aunt Emmy, preoccupied with her illness, seemed to shut him out. Uncle Hugh, like a fortress, was strong, remote and unapproachable. Pam talked only of boys, dancing and dressmaking. George lived for his girl in the Salvation Army. David blamed himself for being out of tune with his new family. They were alright. He was all wrong.

David put his bathing gear under his arm, and no one asked the reason why. At the cricket patch near the elm in the park he told his mates he was going swimming in the afternoon. All they wanted was to get on with the game. The afternoon was too far off to worry about. They would do without him.

The stranger appeared in the same clothes and joined them for lunch. 'Did you ask your aunt and uncle?' he asked David.

'No, but that's alright. They won't mind.' David said.

The man seemed guarded and irritable, and complained of the boys having meat in their sandwiches. He was a vegetarian, he said, and explained what that meant. He had walnut butter on his bread. He offered the boys chocolate, but it was soft and sticky from the heat.

David and the stranger left the other boys ragging on the grass. The man said his name was Arthur. He put David's costume and towel in the panier under the saddle. They used the southern exit into the Kennet valley and pushed off right, away from the town along the Bath Road. They turned left, went over Pigney Bridge, then left again into a quiet lane leading to a large expanse of water trapped in old gravel pits. Arthur, silent and preoccupied, pushed his bike along a rough, broken path skirting the lake.

David had never bathed anywhere except the river and the public baths. Drowned Meadow was a sandy, gravelly wilderness, sun-dried and exposed, without shelter or trees. The lake, still and inert, without tide or flow, and without the cheeky buoyancy of the public baths, seemed like another stranger to David, who felt trapped in that lonely place. The only refuge was the water. The only other humans were a few children engrossed in play, remote, a long way off and out of hearing.

'This will do,' said Arthur, and laid his bike on a patch of rough, weedy grass.

David's costume, thin and faded and with a few holes, contrasted the newish, navy blue woollen one worn by Arthur. A certain tension had kept them both silent, but when they waded into the fresh neutrality of the water they were friends again. Their constraints found release as they swam and broke into the splash and swell of turbulence.

Arthur had a tough, round muscularity, his flesh taut and spare, his baldness fringed with brown and grey hairs round neck and ears. He swam fiercely, then suddenly stopped. 'Come here', he called. 'Let me life-save you.' He bubbled and blew at the surface, then, as David swam towards him, exposed the huge teeth in a smile. 'Relax,' he said. 'Let yourself go limp.'

David felt safe in Arthur's strong and competent hands as he demonstrated his life-saving skills above and below the boy's body. They splashed and played, but, when the big tube lips parted and revealed the teeth, David felt a wave of repulsion. Arthur closed his mouth and blew at the surface of the water. The fun exhausted itself. They came out, dried themselves, and took up the strain again.

David had put on his shirt and was putting on his trousers.

'Before you dress,' Arthur blurted out, 'let me show you how to life-save once more.' He grabbed at David, pulled him down and made leg movements under him. 'That's how you do it,' he said.

David, having learnt what to do in the water, was surprised at having to do the dry exercises as well.

'Now the other way,' Arthur said, and looked athletic standing there in vest and pants. David, lying on the grass, felt a wave of fear. Arthur looked down at his victim, then fell on him face downwards and made violent movements with his legs. He held the boy's chin, pressed his ugly, gristly nose and his blubber lips into his face. Repulsion, horror, like a spring inside him, gave the boy strength to struggle free. He grabbed his things and ran.

David arrived home with his mind in turmoil, and could not speak to Trixie, who followed him into the garden. Compelled by the strain of unhappiness she saw in her cousin's face, she offered the only comfort she could, and dimpled her cheeks into a smile. They wrestled with each other. It loosened all of David's screwed up nerves.

'Is anything the matter?' Trixie asked.

Full of guilt and self-doubt, David gave no answer. For sanctuary, he went into the outside loo and stayed there until Aunt Emmy called him in to tea. Weaving to and fro across the table, a curtain of inconsequential chatter. David hid behind it.

He kept his secret a few days, then, when he was alone with George, made his confession.

'Don't see him again,' George said, and hurried to his girl.

David took possession of the outside loo and yelled until all the members of his foster family hated him for it.

The unique voice of any lamb in a flock of sheep is heard only by its ewe. No shepherd watches twenty-four hours at a stretch. While he sleeps, only the ewe hears the bleating of its lamb, black as pitch, ugly as sin, possibly queer, caught in a wire fence three fields away. She will search all night until she finds it. In summer, when ewes and lambs are separated, their cries keep everyone awake. The concern of the ewe ends only when it is slaughtered. The lamb which cries for its dead ewe cries in vain.

Chapter 10

Having been almost a catamite, he became a cockalorum. In dark green stockings, grey cord breeches with silver side buttons, grey serge coat, leather belt and, under the chin, a white linen band like a bib, David posed for photographs in the back garden under the full glare of the sun. His foster family looked on proudly at his transfiguration, his glory. They had all forgiven his tears and saw him as recovered and going away for his own good on a road to higher things. Trixie, cool in blue gingham, giggled at his sudation in the sun. David, in his moment of bumptious self-satisfaction, stewed in the diaphoratic clobber of school uniform.

For his last few minutes indoors, David cast his coat and slipped from under the magnifying glass. When it was time to go, the women kissed him and the men shook his hand. He picked up his bag, and George led him away.

His Alma Mater, bountiful mother, was, in fact, a man's world of tests, with prizes for success and punishment for failure; a stars and stripes regime in which one might shine, or suffer every form of chastisement and humiliation. Confined, as in a uterus, within a triumvirate of Trustees, Head Master and Head Boy, pupils kicked at the walls of this womb with the growing ferocity of adolescents.

Trustees descended like gods from Olympus, found the school swept and garnished, but did not see the devils waiting to spring when they were gone. The Head Master, appointed the honest Godly and learned man, had the school padre, vicar of St. Edmund's, to assist him in teaching the Catechism in the points of the Christian religion. David told the padre that he had been to the mercy seat at the Salvation Army and all his sins had been washed away in the blood of the Lamb. He could not say whether he had been baptised. 'Never mind,' said the padre, 'we will do you and make sure.' He was a royalist who preached on the martyrdom of King Charles I. All were Laud's men at Sivier's. An image of the Archbishop at prayer, carved in stone, filled a niche of the parish church of St. Edmund's to which the boarders marched morning and evening every Sunday.

This was the bit of mother earth where David grew three years, fed and watered by God's almighty hand. For breakfast, two slices of bread and scrape, a plate of Winnie the cook's porridge, either stiff from too little, or runny from too much water, and a cup of urn-tainted tea. For lunch, a roast on Sunday, cold on Monday, minced on Tuesday, stewed on Wednesday, cold brawn Thursday, boiled fish Friday, and something cheap to end the week. For tea, the same as breakfast without the porridge. For supper, only in winter, a bit of bread and dripping and a cup of cocoa without sugar. Boarders blamed Winnie the cook for every inadequacy and unpalatableness of the diet. She resented this and made them suffer.

Boarders did everything for themselves, sewing, darning their own socks and jerseys, and were divided into four work crews for cleaning the schoolrooms, the lavatories, the dormitories and buttery. Duties changed each week. Punishment for poor work was sifting coal dust. The Head Boy and four monitors, one for each work crew, cracked the whip. It was like Cheese Row, where George was head boy and Andrew and Pat helped keep him in order and stop him doing what he wanted. To his brothers he would always be the baby, the jun, the junior. At Sivier's, however, he could become Head Boy, like Tertius, David thought.

Tertius, the chosen one, having been made perfect, dwelt among the boys and shared their sorrows. Once he was third of three boys with the same name. He was Tertius then, and remained so all his days. David liked him. He behaved like a gentleman and treated seniors and juniors alike. All were equal under the law. He used to strut about the schoolroom learning passages from *Twelfth Night*. Once, David held the text and checked him.

Another of David's heroes was the pupil teacher, Mr. Jackson, called Jacko. Once Head Boy and captain of cricket and football when David first entered the school as a day boy, he scored all the runs and all the goals, but was no academic and struggling to matriculate. Boys teased him, but he clowned good humouredly. He attracted a sequence of pretty girlfriends. They appeared in the park for games, and again on Sunday at St. Edmund's where they hung about the church door for a few words before he marched his charges back to school.

Jacko was just a big boy, like Tertius and the monitors, and like David's older brothers. At Cheese Row he had no allies. He was on his own against authority, but at Sivier's he had Tom Selborne, his contemporary and friend. Tom caught the same tram from Caversham Bridge when the two of them entered the school as day boys, but they had lost touch during the year since David's mother died. They renewed their friendship when they became boarders. Both had been at Sivier's for two years, were neck and neck as scholars, and in the so-called Sixth Form.

Tom, a dark, ungainly rughead with a voracious, undiscriminating appetite, ate everything Winnie cooked, including her Irish stew made from off-cut fat boiled with the remains of Sunday's mutton. This delicacy, carried in a black cauldron, congealed at the surface in the open air on its way from the kitchen to the buttery. The duty master, after giving it a stir, ladelled it into cold, metal plates on which the fat hardened into a yellow crust. David choked with nausea. The rule was that every boy should eat his portion. Tom ate his without a qualm. Surreptitiously, David exchanged his full plate for Tom's empty one. When it was tapioca, Tom had two lots as well. He often had David's porridge too.

Big and awkward, ugly as sin, with a mop of black, unruly hair, Tom Selborne wore thick lens, metal frame spectacles which he broke about a hundred times a term, though he was blind without them. But, when he picked up his black Waterman, how sweetly his thoughts flowed across the page. In the holidays he bought secondhand copies of Edward Gibbon, Lord Macaulay, John Richard Green history books and brought them back to school to read. That is how he learnt his style.

David envied him his style. He and his friend were opposites. He, more the angelic choirboy type with clean trim fingernails, whose stomach heaved when, on buttery duty, he washed the fat encrusted plates in luke warm water which, with only a tiny ration of soda, could not cope with the grease. The smell on his hands disgusted him.

David wanted to write as well as Tom Selborne, but it would not come right. Teachers tore out their hair over his lousy essays. He turned everything into an epic. Always, at the beginning of term, boys had to write about what they did in the holidays. All David ever did was run with steamers, play football and cricket in the park, and go to the twopenny pictures, but he made an Odyssey, a Wembly Cup Final, a Test Match, a Shakespeare tragedy out of them in sentences which were a muddle of inversions, allusions, mixed metaphors, pedantries and God knows what. His essays came back with red ink all over them. When he blubbed it looked like blood. The nicest thing the English master said was that he showed interest. It meant that he did not nod off during the lesson, or bang the desk and throw his books out of the window, like some bully-boy trouble maker.

After these critical reviews, David looked at the picture of his mother and Miss Alice. He worshipped her, his Holy Mother. The Immaculate Conception never troubled him. In the absence of a father he could not imagine anyone, other than his mother, having anything to do with bringing him into this world. She was both creatrix and provider, like Eurynome, Great Mother of the ancient Greeks who, emerging from dark and primitive Chaos, danced with the wind on the waves, turned herself into a Dove and laid the Universal Egg which hatched into the world, the sun and all the stars. Afterwards came Uranus, First Father, Titan wars and the Mother's tears.

Mr. Porter, the Head Master, the Old Man, grey bearded, barrel bellied and bespectacled, ruled Sivier's like the head of a huge Victorian family. Remote, forbidding and unapproachable, he hemmed in his charges with rules, routines and religious observances.

For the boarders, Sunday was a dull day of church services and letter writing, but there were buns for tea. For Winnie the cook it was sufficient that she intended them as a treat. They did not have to be edible as well. Tom Selborne had two, his own and David's. He could have had more. The rest were uneaten. David, on buttery duty, dumped them at the kitchen door.

Winnie, tall, dark and buxom, towered over him. 'What's the meaning of this?' she demanded.

David hesitated. Dare he say it? Speak the truth and shame the devil, he thought. 'They're like chariot wheels,' he said.

Winnie brandished a wooden spoon and drove him away. In a fit of rage she went straight to the Matron and threatened to leave on the spot. Mrs. Porter consulted her husband.

The Old Man took the problem to Evensong at St. Edmund's where he read the lessons and sang in the choir. Thirsting after righteousness, he spent the rest of the night drinking whiskey at The George.

In the dormitories, adolescents bursting with pubertal excitements, talked of their giglets, their desires and longings. Weekends unsettled them. Their girls on the touch line cheered them at football in the park on Saturday afternoon. On Sunday they appeared at church. Stimulated by the sight of their sweethearts, natural forces deep within them erupted when the duty master turned out the lights and left them to themselves. Quietly treading the cold, bare boards, the older boys visited each other for mutual onanistic fulfillment. No warnings of insanity and blindness, no morning sheet inspections staunched these pubescent consolations.

In the middle of the night, long after every boy was asleep, the Old Man came drunkenly with a sack of Winnie's buns. 'Wake up! Wake up!' he stormed, carrying in his other hand an old ship's lantern. He should have been the light of their world. Instead, he sparked and flared like a Lucifer. 'I'll give you chariot wheels, you young shcallywags. Here you are, Have a bun. Put it under your pillow and sleep on it. Warm it up for breakfast in the morning.' He bounced the confections on the dormitory floor, one for each boy, and laughed mischievously, like a boy up to some prank.

At seven o'clock, when it was still dark, young Jacko, drinking early morning tea, roused the boys from slumber. For warmth in the ice cold dormitory, David slept foetal fashion, knees to chin, and woke with aching joints. The exercise of dressing, folding sheets and blankets, sent blood racing and relieved the pain. There were two large dorms, each with twelve beds, and two small ones, each with five. They were separated by two flights of stairs. Jacko went from one dorm to the other, stirring boys into action. As a diversion, boys in David's dorm threw their buns at each other and played football with them. One bun splashed into the slop bucket under the window. 'That will make it soft enough to eat,' said Tom Selborne.

In the buttery the boys sat on wooden benches at bare refectory tables, one on each long wall. After meals these tables were wiped with a cloth wetted in dirty washing-up water. They stank with residual grease. At the draughty end, opposite the only door, the Head Boy and monitors had a small table to themselves. At the other end, the warm end, the Old Man and his wife, and the four resident masters ate at a table laid with linen, damask napkins and silverware.

The boys stood for the Old Man's entrance. He came fierce and silent.

His wife, small and ladylike, with a full, attractive figure neatly dressed, smiled at the boys and said good morning. At her feet came Judy, an old cocker spaniel, waddling, trailing hairs. The Head Boy said grace.

To the Head Master's table a kitchener carried, in silver domed dishes, breakfast fry of bacon, eggs and sausages, and a tray of tea, coffee, toast and marmalade. Smell of fry tickled the boarders taste buds and encouraged feelings of envy and all uncharitableness. They sat down to their bread and scrape and Winnie's buns. Coerced into good behaviour by the presence of their masters, they ate in near silence and listened to the inconsequential chatter of Mrs. Porter. Her chirpy small talk triggered only polite monosyllables and nods from the masters, and a stubborn, head down resentment in her husband.

The Old Man's lumpy, hangover sullenness oppressed masters and boys alike. 'Give it to the dog,' he yelled at his wife.

The spare sausage should have gone to the Head Boy, but he, in disgrace with the rest, had to go without. Mrs. Porter added the sausage to the orts of bone, rind, fat, skin, fried bread collected from the men's plates, and put down the scraps for Judy to eat.

The Old Man rolled his napkin, placed it in its silver ring, and rose to go. The Matron, Judy and the men walked in procession between the refectory tables. The boys rose resentfully and stared at them with hungry eyes. Then they dispersed to their crew duties.

The school bell rang for the calling of the register and morning prayers. Day boys and boarders rushed noisily up the wooden stairs into the large schoolroom, and came guiltily to God, oppressed by preps and duties badly done. The Old Man in cap and gown came solemnly, stood at a small table under the glass partition, adjusted his spectacles, and led the assembly in the Lord's Prayer and the Collect. A boy read the lessons. To the accompaniment of an old upright piano the assembly sang six verses of a psalm, and the Magnificat. The Old Man read the Prayer of St. Chrysostom. There was a closing hymn and a blessing.

Boys disappeared to their respective Forms. In the Sixth Form David sat in a double desk with Tom Selborne. Mr. Horn, the senior master, glided in. His black gown billowed behind him. He had the airy lightness of a bird of prey. His face was aquiline, high cheek-boned, osseous and sallow. This thin faced, melancholy man taught mathematics and science with authority. Boys respected him.

The Old Man, bad tempered after his drunken night, sat at a desk in front of the long, wall blackboard. There he attended to correspondence and examined full exercise books. The arrangement was bad for everybody. Pupils, fearing his explosions at wrong answers, hated him there. Teachers resented the close, on-the-spot surveillance of their lessons. There he sat, his hands and face splotchy red, his bald head postulous and flaky. He wore a black skull cap to hide the disintegration of his scalp. Scratching, then withdrawing a clawed finger, left the cap askew and gave him a tipsy look.

Mr. Horn enthused with the truths of Pythagoras and mathematical relationships. On the wall board, which extended the width of the room, he chalked circles, triangles and squares.

Suddenly, the Old Man interrupted with a roar. 'Stand up, Sedgewick,' he yelled, and held up a book of David's essays. His angry eyes glared behind the gold rimmed spectacles. 'Stinks with conceit!' he shouted, and threw the book at his victim. 'Write out one hundred times 'I must not write above the line'.'

Mr. Horn showed no embarrassment or resentment at this disturbance. The two maintained a silent antipathy and rarely spoke to each other in public. Any necessary discussion of school affairs took place behind closed doors. Although he treated his superior with a quiet, deferential contempt, Mr. Horn maintained the Old Man's authority, and insisted on obedience to his commands. Other teachers came and went, but Mr. Horn stayed on, a figure of stability in that ailing academy.

Appropriately, after the Old Man's ferments, Mr. Horn, in the physics lesson which followed mathematics, instructed his pupils in Boyle's Law concerning the relationship of gas, temperature and pressure.

At the mid-morning break David suffered the innocent raillery of his class mates. 'Pooh! What a pong!' one of them cried, and held his nostrils. They called him 'Smeller' and 'Stink Pot'. Tom Selborne called him 'Savoury Dave.' The teasing was without malice. Each boy knew he might be the next to suffer public ignominy. The fun eased David's chagrin; neutralised the poison of fear and insecurity at his roots.

'Let's play some footer,' Tom Selborne said, and, in the vast gravel play area, they joined a crowd kicking away grudges on an old tennis ball. Others played tip-cat at a structure of old railway sleepers set up as a rifle range during the war. Some swung on a pair of rickety, splintery parallel bars. Bigger boys exercised with a medicine ball, heavy as lead, and, for fun, knocked down little ones standing by.

The school bell rang for the end of play.

Mr. Gregory, known as 'Pope', tall and plump, long nosed, and with a mole which sprouted from his high complexioned, shiny face, sailed into the Sixth Form. He was substituting for Mr. Conway, the regular history master, and was the last of a succession of barely qualified, badly paid temporary teachers at Sivier's. He carried a stack of heavy volumes under his arm to impress the pupils with the weight of his learning. His method of teaching was to read directly from these textbooks. He did this not entirely from ignorance, but because of a lack of confidence to sustain anything impromptu for the duration of a lesson.

The Old Man sat at his desk and kept the boys orderly. He had long ago seen through the pretentions of the 'Pope'. Still in aggressive mood, he sat waiting to pounce while the temporary toiled in his attempt to conceal his inadequacies. Suddenly the Old Man interrupted. 'John Richard Green, I believe, Mr. Gregory. A great historian. I know the passage well. Would you like me to finish it for you?' He glared above the rim of his spectacles.

Mr. Gregory heightened colour and was speechless with guilt and confusion.

'Please finish reading the lesson,' the Old Man said mischievously. 'Or get one of the boys to read it for you.'

The Old Man left the classroom. The lesson wasted itself in uproar.

Tom Selborne opened his desk, took out his own copy of *A Short History of the English People* by John Richard Green, and found the passage at which the Old Man interrupted. He turned to David and chuckled. 'He's right, you know, the old bugger,' he said. 'I don't know which is funnier. The lesson we've had, or the one we're going to have.'

The Old Man had left the classroom to welcome the padre, who took the Catechism for the last period of Monday morning school. The Old Man did not come back. The padre restored order and gave another history lesson on the martyrdom of King Charles I and the Divine Right of Kings. The Episcopalian Church of England was the one true faith. Everyone should be baptised. We were all conceived in sin and must be born of Water and the Holy Ghost.

Before he went, the padre signed the Visitors Book which lay open on the Head Master's desk. Page after page of it recorded nothing but a column of dates and the padre's signatures. The signing had become a ritual. Boys crowded the man of God for affection, and he cuddled them.

David and Tom Selborne remained in their seats.

'What a load of codswallop,' said Tom.

'What?' asked David

'That Catechism,' said Tom.

'Why?'

'Men and women are supposed to be made in the image of God, aren't they?'

'That's right.'

'Your mum and dad were made in the image of God.'

'Of course.'

'How could you be born in sin?'

'I don't know,' said David. 'I hadn't thought about it.'

'Think about it, then. And what's so wonderful about water?'

'You wash in it. It makes you clean.'

'Soap makes you clean. Water doesn't take the grease off plates after Winnie's stew. Besides, you can drown in it.'

'You can drink it,' said David. 'There's nothing like a glass of cold water on a hot day.'

'If it's not treated, it poisons you,' said Tom.

The bell rang for lunch.

The padre, like Winnie's buns, was a left-over from Sunday. He and Mrs. Porter made a joint effort at good tempered conversation, but lunch, like breakfast, was eaten in an atmosphere of inhibited, taciturn gloom.

The bell rang for afternoon school.

Mr. Conway, sturdy and handsome, called 'Curly' because of his dark, wavy, unoiled hair brushed back without a parting, taught the subjects David liked. He waited for the boys to settle. 'Take out your Shakespeare and Dickens,' he said. 'And do it quietly without banging your desks.'

The Old Man rarely appeared in the afternoon. The English master had his pupils to himself. The boys did as they were told, quietly, and took out their copies of *Richard II* and *The Tale of Two Cities*.

Mr. Conway also taught history, and teased out what the boys knew of the reign of Richard II; his foreign wars; the poll tax and the Lollards; the discontents of the poor; Watt Tyler's rebellion and the forcing of the Tower; the murder of the Archbishop; the quarrels of the king and nobles; the fall of Richard II. He wrapped the ends of his gown in front of him, projected his lower jaw, rolled his tongue as though relishing the flavour of his subject, and asked Tom Selborne, the bookworm of the class, if he knew the poem known as *The Complaint of Piers Ploughman.*

'Yes, sir,' said Tom. 'It was written by William Langland and describes the miseries of the poor in the fourteenth century.'

'Good,' said Mr. Conway. 'It is an Anglo-saxon classic, like Chaucer's *Canterbury Tales.* Many other similar poems were written, but they were shorter. More like popular songs, or the spirituals of American negroes.' He opened a book in front of him. 'Listen to this, he said.

Falseness and guile have reigned too long,
and truth hath been set under a lock,
and falseness and guile reigneth in every stock.
No man may come truth to,
but if he sing 'si dedero'.
True love is away that was so good,
and clerks for wealth work them woe.
God do bote, for now is tyme.

The teacher repeated the last line and explained its meaning. God will put things right, and now is the time. 'For now is tyme.' He stressed each word to impress the phrase on his pupils minds. 'Now I want you to turn to Chapter XVI in Book the Second of *The Tale of Two Cities* he said, and enfolded himself in his gown, projected his lower jaw, rolled his tongue, then asked David to read the passage in which Defarge complains to his wife that the revolution is taking too long a time.

'It is a long time' repeated his wife, 'and when is it not a long time? Vengeance and retribution require a long time; it is the rule.'

'It does not take a long time to strike a man with lightning' said Defarge.

'How long' demanded madame composedly, 'does it take to make and store the lightning? Tell me.'

Defarge raised his forehead thoughtfully, as if there were something in that, too.

'It does not take long' said madame, 'for an earthquake to swallow a town. Eh, well! Tell me how long it takes to prepare an earthquake.'

'A long time, I suppose' said Defarge.

'But when it is ready, it takes place, and grinds to pieces everything before it. In the meantime, it is always preparing, though it is not seen nor heard. This is your consolation. Keep it.'

Mr. Conway allowed time for the passage to sink in. 'Now boys,' he said. 'Do you see history repeating itself? The forcing of the Tower of London in the reign of Richard II and the storming of the Bastille in the French Revolution. Try and remember that wonderful image of Madame Defarge. The forces of nature building up and, at the right time, releasing enormous energy in lightning and earthquake. Like the forces of discontent breaking out, at the appropriate moment, to restore the balance between rich and poor.'

In the pause which followed, the boys made their connections. There was the violence of nature, and there was the violence of man.

'Please, sir,' asked David.

'Yes, what is it?'

'Please, sir, was the Great War like that sir? You know, sir, when the Archduke was assassinated at Sarajevo?'

'A very good parallel,' said Mr. Conway. 'Europe was like a barrel of gunpowder, the assassination triggered off its explosion.'

He beamed with satisfaction, like a man replete, anticipating brandy. 'Put your books away and take out your Milton,' he said.

At the end of the lesson the two friends spoke to each other behind the flaps of their desks as they were putting their books away.

'Do you believe that story about Satan rebelling against God?' David asked.

'I don't believe in God or Satan,' Tom Selborne said, 'it's a load of codswallop.'

'What do you believe in?'

'The Russian Revolution,' said Tom, and laughed. 'Up the Reds!' he shouted, and banged his desk in defiance of the rules.

There was no bell for Dr. Martin, who came every Monday afternoon after lessons and took a choir practice in the large schoolroom. David enjoyed singing and looked forward to the practices, the Monday one and the one on Thursday evening when the boarder choristers marched down to St. Edmund's to sing with the men.

Through the week thoughts, like threads, of guilt, fear, isolation, inadequacy, twisted like knots in his brain. On Sunday the knots unravelled in the rhythms of the King James bible, the Book of Common Prayer, the Psalms and Canticles. The sacred music flowed like life-blood and healed his wounds. Dr. Martin noticed David's genuine enthusiasm and promoted him quickly in the stalls.

The white haired Doctor, small and neat, stood behind the piano and banged out the hymns and psalms for the following Sunday. To keep tempo, and indicate the correct pointing of the psalms, he nodded vigorously from over the top of the piano. Occasionally he stopped abruptly to correct wrong notes.

After the practice, Dr. Martin gave David a piano lesson. To start with, all the scales. Then the Doctor played a simple *Courante* by Bach. When David attempted it he fumbled the notes. The Doctor, without warning, knocked up his hands from the keys and found them tight and tense. 'Relax. Loosen up,' he said.

David liked the gentle doctor and was over-anxious to please. This added to his other complexes and made him clumsy. Failure turned him into a cry-baby and he could not read the music for tears.

'Are you still worrying about this morning?' Dr. Martin asked.

David, guessing the Old Man had told him he stank with conceit, could not speak.

'Never mind,' said the Doctor. 'Sing to me.'

Doctor Martin accompanied, and David sang *Fairest Isle*.

'Lovely,' said the Doctor. 'Practise the *Courante* and show me how well you can play it next week. Watch the fingering.'

David went happily away.

When the Doctor left, the schoolroom exploded with noise. One boy had a portable gramophone with only one record, *Bye, Bye, Blackbird*, which he played over and over again. Two boys set up an improvised arrangement of three blackboards side by side on top of the desks and played ping-pong. The ball hit the cracks between the boards and bounced away at unpredictable angles. The contestants disputed these points and banged their bats on the boards to reinforce their arguments. Other boys banged the flaps of desks and the doors of their lockers. These lockers, one for each boarder, used for storing tuck and other articles, ran the length of the schoolroom under a long, fitted window seat either side of the central fireplace. Above the seat, under the windows, portraits of Head Boys looked quietly down out of their frames at the mayhem below. Tertius strutted about with *Twelfth Night*, then left the schoolroom for a breath of fresh air.

Tom Selborne sat alone at his desk in the sixth form, absorbed in Macaulay's *History of England*, and did not look up when David joined him and took out *Les Miserables*. Selborne wrapped himself round the desk, knocked his knees together in a regular rhythm and lulled himself into a dream world centuries old.

Suddenly, three ruffians shattered Selborne's dream. Resentful of the barrier of intelligent absorption behind which Tom isolated himself, they dragged him from the desk and pulled him about the schoolroom. His spectacles fell to the floor. David picked them up and put them safely away. Selborne, head down, uncomplaining, asking no mercy, dribbled at the mouth.

Tertius returned. The hectoring stopped. The two friends resumed their reading.

The bell rang for tea.

By a system of 'bagging', boarders secured from each other scraps like the core of an apple, the last broken remnants of a bag of potato crisps, the last mouthful of a bottle of mineral water. When Winnie cooked a roast, the first boy to approach the duty master who carved, could bag the knuckle meat if it was mutton, or the outside brown of the top cut if it was beef. For tea, Tom Selborne was knifing out the last full helping of his mother's home made blackcurrant jam, and spreading it on his two slices of bread and scrape.

'Bags the bottom,' David said.

Tom handed over the jam jar. David scratched the last smears of sweetness from it to help down the slice of bread. The other slice he gave to Tom, who ate it as it was, with nothing on it.

The bell rang for prep.

Young Jacko, who needed the prep as much as the pupils, drew up a chair and sat at a small table in front of the Old Man's desk in the sixth form.

After prep, boarders rushed to the buttery for a cup of Winnie's unsweetened cocoa and a slice of bread and dripping which they consumed in the schoolroom while the duty crew swept the floors for the morning. Afterwards they talked, played, quarrelled until bed at 8.30.

'Carrots,' the most junior of the three boys who had bullied Tom Selborne, approached David and called him a milksop. David called him a lout.

'Watch it, stinker,' said Carrots. 'I'll have the pants off you.' He had a solid, bouncy muscularity and a shiny, button-nosed pugnaciousness which David disliked.

David felt brave. 'You couldn't knock the skin off a rice pudding,' he said.

'I'll knock you into the middle of next week if you don't shut up,' said Carrots.

Boys gathered, some of them victims of Carrots bullying, but all of them remembering David's humiliation that morning. One of them held his nose in front of David and said 'Pooh! Who farted?' Another said 'Go on, Dave, give him one', but ran away when Carrots threatened him with clenched fists.

'Want to try it, then, shrimp?' challenged Carrots, determined on provocation. He pretended to wave a stink from under his nose. 'Smells like rotten fish,' he said.

The small boys looked at David. He was not much bigger than they were, but he could not let them down. 'Come on, then,' he said.

A ring of boys enclosed the combatants. David had no chance. It was like fighting his mother's mangle. Everything he hit was hard. He closed in to wrestle. Carrots squeezed him like a wet cloth. Kids cheered David, but all his breath was gone. There was a sudden quiet. Jacko saved him.

'You will both be reported to the Head Master,' the pupil teacher said, and parted the contestants. 'You know what that means, don't you?'

In the morning they were caned in the tuck-shop. At mid-morning break, before the whole school, they fought three two-minute rounds with bare fists on the lawn in the angle between the old house and the school. Who won? There was no referee and no decision, but David knew alright. He was no champ. His only satisfaction was that he had met a challenge.

Chapter 11

On Armistice Day, masters and monitors harangued work crews and searched out crumbs, litter, dusty ledges and dirty windows. When all was swept and garnished, masters and boys assembled in the large schoolroom. Old Boys filed in solemnly. Some wore poppies. Some wore medals. Their president placed a wreath of poppies on the shelf of a memorial plaque above the fireplace. They sang *For All the Saints who from their Labours Rest*. David thought proudly of his mother and father with their crowns of gold. 'Greater love hath no man than this, that he lay down his life for his friend.' Guns fired. Silence muffled the room like a blanket of snow. A fly, dozy from sleep, disturbed by a boy with a duster, buzzed and fell. A rook called. The wind sighed. David strayed from remembrance. Then, making a conscious effort to keep his mind fixed on his father, he imagined him bleeding in the snow, shot by a sniper. Boys coughed. The fire under the wreath whispered its secrets. Guns fired. David felt guilty that all his thoughts had not been of his father. 'They shall not grow old as we that are left grow old.' The words carried him along on a current of emotion. No questions curled in his brain. He saluted with the rest, and the Old Boys marched away.

In the hour before tea, Mr, Conway, duty master, sat at the long, rexine covered table near the piano and marked exercise books. David hesitated to intrude, the events of Armistice Day preyed on his mind. He wanted to show his memorabilia to Mr. Conway.

'Is there something you wish to say to me?' Mr. Conway asked.

'Please, sir, would you like to look at these, sir?'
The teacher closed an exercise book and added it to one of the piles.
'What are they?' he asked.
'Just a few souvenirs, sir.'
'Show me.'
David handed him the Mons Star, the East Surrey Christmas card with
their battle honours, the French blue bead necklace and cross, and the
picture of his father fraternising with French soldiers in Jersey before the
war.
'So your father was in the East Surreys?'
'The 1st East Surreys, sir. He was a sergeant, sir.'
'It has a long history and a fine reputation.'
'I know, sir. My dad was proud of his regiment, sir.'
'It was part of the BEF. The British Expeditionary Force. The Old
Contemptibles.'
'Sir?'
'The Old Contemptibles. They were called that because the German
Kaiser said that the BEF was a contemptible little army. He meant that it
was too small to be of any use in France. It is true, there were not many
of them, but the soldiers were very brave, and bore the brunt of the
fighting in the first few months of the war.'
'Sir?'
'It was a little bit like football. France and Belgium was the pitch. The
Germans made a strong attack down their right wing. If the British
soldiers had not defended strongly on the Allied left, the Germans might
have scored a goal and taken Paris. Do you understand?'
'I think so, sir. Thank-you, sir.'
Mr. Conway returned the mementoes and started marking again.
Tom Selborne came over to look at David's treasures. 'Sir?' he said.
'Yes, what is it?'
'War is evil, isn't it, sir?'
'Those who start wars are often evil.'
'They cause a lot of suffering, don't they, sir?' said David.
'That's right.'
'Please, sir, what about earthquakes which swallow up whole towns,
sir?' asked Tom.
'Well,' said Mr. Conway, 'you can't blame anyone for earthquakes.
They just happen because of the way the earth is made.'
'Sir?' said Tom.

'Yes, what is it?'

'God made the earth, didn't he, sir?' asked Tom.

'That's what the Bible says, my boy.'

'Sir, would you think earthquakes have killed as many people as wars, sir?' asked Tom.

'You are getting on shaky ground, my boy. The problem of suffering is a difficult one. Christians believe that God entered into the suffering of the world when Jesus was crucified.'

Mr. Conway, indicating his reluctance to continue the debate, took another exercise book for marking.

The two boys walked away, and David returned the souvenirs to his locker.

At the beginning of evening prep Mr. Conway, carrying a red book in his hand, approached David. 'The medal you showed me this afternoon was the Mons Star,' he said.

'Yes, sir.'

'I thought you might like to read an account of the Retreat from Mons. Your father must have taken part in it.'

The history master indicated a passage and asked David to take it away and read it. By the 5th September 1914 the BEF had retreated two hundred miles from the Mons Canal. An officer said it was difficult to believe that men could be so tired and hungry and yet live. They marched for thirteen days with only four hours rest each day. The troops suffered every disadvantage. Reservists, of whom David's father was one, made up half the strength. They had been hurried into battle without preparation, to fight superior numbers of the best trained army in Europe. In the battle for Mons, and in the retreat, they were short of food and sleep, but never demoralised, because they had never been beaten.

When David returned the book, Mr. Conway directed his attention to another part of the text. 'I think you need a little extra French prep,' he said. 'Translate this passage into English for me. You may find it difficult, but don't worry. Let me know if you need any help.'

General Joffre's Congratulatory Telegram – 27 August 1914 Commandant en Chef des Armées Françaises a Commandant en Chef Armée Anglaise Noyon Oise. No. 2425. L'Armée Anglais en n'hésitant pas à s'engage tout entière contre des forces supérieures en nombre a puissement contribué a assurer la securité du flanc gauche de l'Armée Française. Elle l'a fait avec devouement, une énergie et une perseverance auxquels Je tiens des maintenant a rendre hommage et qui se retrouveront demain pour assurer le triomphe final de la cause commune. L'Armée Française n'oublière le service rendu; animée du même esprit de sacrifice et de même colonté de vaincre que L'Armée Anglaise, elle lui affirme sa reconaissance, dans les prochaine combats.

> Joffre.

On the Festival of All Saints, David, dry throated, stepped out of the choir stalls at St. Edmund's, stood under the rood and sang from Brahms *German Requiem*.

> And ye now therefore have sorrow:
> but I will see you again,
> and your heart shall rejoice,
> and your joy no man taketh from you.
> As one whom his mother comforteth
> so will I comfort you.
> Behold with your eyes,
> how that I laboured but a little,
> and found for myself much rest.

Spring term started in ice cold winter. David's croak attracted the attention of Mrs. Porter, who sent for the doctor. He was ordered to bed in the warm isolation of the San. The lofty little room was filled with light from two windows on opposite walls. It had only two beds, the other one empty. The boy had two fires, one in the grate, the other burning inside him. In the long, dark evenings, he stared at the flames, then at the shadows dancing on the wall. When he coughed it was like a dog barking at children as they play. Thoughts came frantically, like flies, bees, birds, butterflies trapped, beating their wings against a window where they see freedom, but can find no way through. At eight o'clock a small boy came, dampened the fire and went away. The wall dance ceased but David's bark continued. A demon, lurking in slimy trails along the corridors of the thorax, would not let him sleep.

In the morning Mr. Horn came noiselessly. He had no Christian sympathy for the weak. Occasionally, when there was no one else to do it, he taught Scripture, but his heart was never in it, and he presented the Gospels as dry record, not as testaments of living faith. In church he remained dumb for prayers, hymns, psalms, creed, and sat stubbornly upright when all around him knelt in silent reverent worship. In mathematics and physics he showed how things worked by logical and mechanical rules. Not for him the possibility of intervention by a transcendent God, or the belief that the meek would inherit the earth. As games master he displayed a nimble athleticism at football, and opened the bowling at cricket. Once, when David kept wicket, he sent down a ball which whipped past bat and stumps, through the keeper's gloves into his stomach, and knocked the lad out. While David writhed on the grass, Mr. Horn, calmly indifferent, looked down on his agony.

Mr. Horn drifted in and sat on the bed. 'Tell me, can you hear yourself breathing?' he asked, and stroked his long, bony, rudder nose. His expression showed an impassive control, as though distancing himself. The purpose of his visit, it seemed, was to make a scientific enquiry.

'Yes, sir. It keeps me awake.'

'I know. The wheezing. It's horrible,' Mr. Horn said, and, with an answer to his question, seemed ready to go.

'Was that the gas, sir?'

'What do you know about the gas?'

'That's what the boys say, sir. That you were gassed in the war.'

'Do they now. And what else do they say?'

'Nothing, sir. The war must have been horrible, sir.'

'The next one will be worse.'

'Sir?'

'You should read *The War of the Worlds* by H.G. Wells. It tells you just what the wars of the future will be like.'

'Will there be another war, sir?'

'I hope not, but, you see, the government has to plan to defend the country in case we are attacked. That's why we build warships and weapons. Aeroplanes played only a small part in the last war, but in the next they will be able to drop bombs powerful enough to wipe out whole cities. Each country keeps its own secret weapons. Then something happens, and before we know it we are at war again.'

'I know, sir, like the assassination of the Archduke at Sarajevo. It's like lightning and earthquake, isn't it, sir?' Terrific forces waiting to break out when the time comes.'

'Yes, it's a bit like that, but you have to remember we can't prevent earthquakes, whereas it should be possible to prevent wars.'

'Sir?'

'Yes, what is it?'

'Could the Great War have been prevented, sir?'

'Possibly not. The causes went back a very long way.'

'We had to beat the Kaiser, didn't we, sir?'

'Once you are in a war, you have to win it.'

'Sir?'

'What is it now?' Mr. Horn asked with an air of long suffering.

'You always win if you fight for a good cause, don't you, sir?'

'Not necessarily. In the Great War the Allies won because, in the end, the Americans joined and made us superior in men and weapons. You are studying *Paradise Lost* aren't you? Do you remember how the angel Gabriel intimidates Satan? I wonder if I can remember the lines.

'. . .read thy lot in yon celestial sign
Where thou art weighed, and shown how light, how weak,
If thou resist. . .'

'You see,' Mr. Horn continued, warming a little to his subject, 'Satan thought his cause was just, but Gabriel warned him that the Scales would show how, if the opposing forces were weighed against each other, he was too weak to win. It is another version of the survival of the fittest.'

'Sir?'

'I know what you're thinking, my boy, that God had to win because the cause was right, but I think what Milton is really saying is that God, who he believed could harness the forces of the universe, would always win against an underling whose weapons were less strong.'

'You mean, like earthquakes, sir?'

'Earthquakes and many other forces locked up in the universe.'

'Sir?'

'More questions, my boy?'

'Sir, will you tell us about earthquakes sometime, sir?'

'Well, my boy,.I didn't come here to talk about war and earthquakes. You are a very earnest young man, aren't you? Mr. Conway showed me your essay on the school motto. I notice you are still writing above the line. You'll be in trouble again if you're not careful. I've been trying not to believe what the Headmaster said about you being conceited, but you have some very airy-fairy ideas about truth, I must say. It's good having two boys like you and Selborne who take a real interest in such subjects, but you should not be too pious and high-horse about it all.'

'Sir?'

'Don't be so dreamy. Keep your feet on the ground. Try not to go overboard so much. What is truth, anyway?'

'Sir?'

'It is the question Pilate asked, and would not stay for an answer. There is no answer. There are too many mysteries. You will find as you get older, my boy, that truth is a good servant but a bad master.'

The remark made a hole in David's well. His essay had been all for truth, the great light, the ultimate reality, the end of faith. God is Love. That truth should be the guiding principle of life. How could it be a bad master?

Mr, Horn stroked his nose and gave David a searching look. He got up from the bed. 'I hope you are soon better,' he said. 'You'll have a lot to catch up with when you get back to school.' He walked noiselessly away. Even in the warm stillness of the San, he seemed to float on a current of air. His black gown billowed behind him.

When the fires burned out Mrs. Porter put him in Thermogen and sent him back to school. The stuff, like pink cotton wool, had a pleasant, feminine smell which reminded David of his mother. Mrs. Porter wrapped it round his chest like a girl's bodice. It gave his mates another excuse for mockery and banter. Matron dosed him on cod-liver oil, milky-white, evil smelling and tasting stuff, not a bit like the treacly, malty medicine his mother used to give him. Soon, he was playing football again and scoring goals.

At the end of term, all exams over for the year, teachers welcome the chance to relax and talk on subjects outside the syllabus. In the sixth form, Mr. Horn asked for suggestions.

David put up his hand. 'Please, sir, would you tell us about earthquakes, sir?'

Mr. Horn lifted his sleeve and looked at his watch. He had the class to himself, so he sat on the corner of the Old Man's desk and resigned himself to the task. Swinging his legs backwards and forwards from the knees, stroking his bony nose, he said that in China, in the sixteenth century, a million people were killed in an earthquake.

The boys gasped.

Mr. Horn continued, swinging his legs in circles. The Chinese regarded an earthquake as a portent of change – a revolution, perhaps, and a new line of emperors. They invented the seismograph based on the principle of the pendulum. Disturbance of the earth's surface caused a tilting mechanism to push out little balls through the mouths of dragons round the top of a vase into the mouths of china frogs round its base.

The science master got off the desk and walked to the blackboard. He described two huge chalk circles and created the world. Drawing diagrams on the blackboard was something he did well. With confident, flowing movements of the arm he drew first one semi-circle, then another to meet it. He told the class that in San Francisco in 1906 an earthquake killed seven hundred people.

The boys gasped again.

The Americans started to research the causes of earthquakes, and someone came up with the theory that they occur at ruptures, or faults in the earth's crust. The teacher returned to the blackboard, sketched the continents, and with pink chalk, indicated the lines of the faults. Then he resumed his seat and said, earthquakes were caused by the disintegration of the earth's crust. When one section, or plate, slid under another, the waves of movement from the centre of disturbance shook the upper crust of the earth. They may cause death and devastation over a wide area. Sometimes, molten matter is forced up into a volcanic eruption which, if it happens on the ocean bed, can result in the formation of new islands. Release of the enormous energy provides a balance between disintegration and stability.

All this worried David. Could it happen in England, he asked. Mr. Horn was ready with the answer. At Colchester, in 1884, four people were killed by an earthquake. Could such disasters be prevented? asked Tom Selborne. No, but it might be possible, one day, to forecast when they would occur. The forces were too remote and powerful for man to control. He dismissed the class with a wave of the hand.

David and Tom Selborne remained in their seats.

'The earth is a dangerous place,' Tom said.

'It must be terrible, buried alive,' David said.

'The sparrows are alright,' Tom said. 'God looks after them. I suppose they fly out of the way.'

'Every hair is numbered,' David said.

'Fat lot of good that is if you're squashed under a stone,' Tom said.

Both of them had learnt these quotations for the religious knowledge exam. Tom's familiarity with scripture meant nothing more than that. He had dodged Confirmation, calling it a nonsense and a delusion. David was more gullible. He believed the promises of the Magnificat, the Holy Mother's song, that God would put down the mighty, exalt the humble and feed the hungry. And the assurance in the Psalms that God defends the fatherless and widowed. Tom told him to watch out, the pledges might not be honoured. David even found comfort in the Litany, which covered every contingency of human failure. Tom told him not to be daft, because in all the centuries it had been recited the world was no better for it. It did not shake David's faith. The complications of the Trinity were no worse than Euclid. He regarded the Creed, in any of its forms, as a statement of truth no less than Pythagoras, recited each with equal conviction, and accepted what he could not understand. By his Baptism and Confirmation, David believed he would be strengthened daily by the Holy Ghost, the Comforter, in wisdom and understanding. The Bishop, in mitre and cloth of gold, swung his crook like a magician, lifted a diamante cloth, laid his hands on him and asked the Lord to defend him with heavenly Grace.

At the end of term feasting in the dorms, David sang with his companions.

This time next week where shall we be?
Outside the gates of misery.
No more drinking out of dirty mugs.
No more cabbage chopped up with slugs.
Pull old Conway by the hairs,
Throw the Horn down the stairs.
If the Old Man interferes,
Knock him down and box his ears.

He had expected Sivier's, with its motto on truth, to solve mysteries. Instead, the enigmas increased. Could Edgar Wallace help? *The Four Just Men*, *The Crimson Circle*, *The Green Archer*. The detectives, hunting villains, solving mysteries, temporarily held his interest, but left him still puzzled, so he abandoned them and searched under the covers of other books to find a way out of his dilemmas.

Intending them as guides to boarding school life, George had given him *St. Winifred's* and Dean Farrar's *Eric or Little by Little*. They filled his eyes. Blinded him with tears. He identified with all the tragic, hunted characters of fiction. Above all, Sydney Carton, that sad loser. In *Les Miserables* he ran side by side with Jean Valjean through the Paris sewers.

For the Oxford locals, Mr. Conway straightened his back, enclosed himself in his gown, rolled his tongue, and contrasted the characters of *Rob Roy* and *The Merchant of Venice*; Shylock the jew, the outsider, the usurer of the Rialto, and Macgregor the outlaw living by plunder in the Scottish Highlands. Both were pariahs, hunted men with whom David sympathised.

He approached the rexine covered table where Mr. Conway was marking exercise books.

'Yes, what is it?' said the English master, looking up.

'Sir, my mother was a Scot, sir, like Rob Roy.'

'There are a good many Scots in the world,' Mr. Conway said, and smiled, as though to say there was nothing remarkable about that.

'Her family name was Tulloch, sir.'

Mr. Conway, who had started marking again, put down his pencil and looked thoughtfully into space. 'That's interesting,' he said. 'I think the Tullochs are related to the Grants. I once read a story about a character called Dusky Black John. He was a Macgregor like Rob Roy and played the fiddle. The king's men were hunting him down when he found refuge in the barn of the Grants of Tullochgorm. The daughter of the laird found him and they fell in love. The soldiers tracked him down while they were dancing together. The lovers stood back to back, she with his dirk, he with his sword, and beat them off. Afterwards, they danced *The Reel of Tulloch*.'

Aunt Emmy kept her secret too long and did not give the doctors a chance. In the spring, when she went into hospital, David went back to Aunt Annie. The family had moved, and he found himself transplanted to a house at the rag and bone yard where Uncle Dick was foreman. Andrew went too.

On a hot summer afternoon, Aunt Annie took David to see Aunt Emmy in hospital. Boiling in full uniform, overcome by the smells of the ward, he fainted. A nurse took him away and revived him with a glass of water. He never went to say goodbye.

Then Gran died, and David, at the old house in Cheese Row, saw her in the open coffin and came, once again, face to face with the sadness of the world.

Waste surrounded the house. Bones from butchers, abbatoirs, knackers, had bits of meat adhering to them. The stench of rotting flesh, worse when summer came, attracted rats, big, brown, long-tailed scavengers. In the evening, after working hours, they took over and ran amok, in and out of piles of old rags, papers and refuse.

The house fronted a busy street. The family ate in the front basement, the only natural light of which came from a window under an iron grating let into the public pavement. Pedestrians struck the iron bars at all hours of the day and night and turned the grid into a bell which tolled endlessly for unknown dead. David escaped this dungeon when Uncle Dick persuaded his lorry drivers to take him on delivery and collection trips to depots in London and the Home Counties. Journeys started at daybreak and often ended after dark.

Stairs led up from the basement kitchen to the ground floor parlours. Behind the stairs a basement coal store opened on to a small enclosure with a gate to the yard. There was no garden. Rats strayed from the yard to the enclosure, then into the basements of the house, and could be heard knawing under the stairs. Aunt Annie, frightened to death, screamed, and complained bitterly to Uncle Dick, whose only weapon was a stick. Poison had been laid, but the rats came on. The few which died added to the stink of the yard.

Aunt Annie's heart condition got worse. The attacks came more frequently. David hated seeing her so ill, so dark and beautiful and tall and pale where she stood, sipping brandy and gripping the mantelpiece while Uncle Dick held and rubbed her into temporary relief. Greta Garbo and John Gilbert, Al Jolson in the new talkies, for whom she wore a skull hat over her shingled hair and ear lobes, distracted her from the rats and the pain.

Esther, frail and petite, her red hair about her tiny, pretty face, remained sunny with affection. The two cousins, left alone, came together and kissed.Then he remembered the words of the Catechism and convinced himself of sin. The padre had never attempted to explain the unmentionable enigma. Young catechumen had to muddle along and puzzle it out for themselves. David needed a mercy seat for confession, and the consolation of an old friend at his side, clasping his shoulder, calming his anxieties concerning the pleasure he felt in his crutch. The General Confession did not work. It left him condemning his cock without knowing why, if he had been made in the image of God, his member offended so persistently. Why should he feel so ashamed of the body God had given him?

Alone in the house, waiting for Esther, David heard the rats below stairs and felt a gnawing in his loins. He went into the front parlour, sat at the piano and practised the chromatic scale, running up and down, fast and furious, driving out desire.

When Esther came she had a companion. There, with his cousin, was Diana. Dumb with self-doubt, bewildered by the urges of his body, he treated Diana like a stranger. Muddying the clear pool of her eyes, he slunk out of doors.

When he returned Diana was gone.

Esther was cool. 'You're a fine one, treating her like that,' she said. 'I thought you'd be pleased to see her.'

'I'm sorry,' David said. 'It was such a shock.'

'Do you still like her?'

'Of course.'

'More than me?'

'It's different,' said David, and looked puzzled. 'I like you a lot.' David hesitated. 'Oh, I don't know,. I can't make it out. Why is she back?'

'Her father's given up the Salvation Army. He didn't like moving about. It upset the family too much.'

'Why didn't they stay in Wolverhampton?'

'They didn't like it there. They decided to come back to Reading. Diana is at my school. She started at the beginning of term. We got talking. She told me she knew you. You were sweethearts, she said.'

David remembered. He was happy then, when his mother was alive. At his junior school, before he left to go to Sivier's, he appeared in a classroom photograph. Of the forty-three boys in the picture, he stood out as the only one smiling. Since then, the smile had been wiped off his face. He and Diana had grown apart. She, Salvationist and Puritan, and he, indoctrinated Episcopalian and Royalist. Too much had happened since that moment of innocent wonder when they collapsed into each other's arms. Only a time machine, an instrument of magic, could help them recapture that emotion, free and urgent as the salmon's leap.

The 'Pope' did not come back for the summer term. The Old Man stepped in and took some lessons himself. The pupils of all three forms crowded into the large schoolroom. Mr. Porter stood in front of the fireplace and spoke to them of the romanticism of Schuman, Chopin, Mendelsshon. He explained the German *Lied* and Song Cycles – *A Poet's Love* and *Woman's Love of Life*. The Old Man taught with great authority and conviction, and persuaded the boys that once upon a time he had been a young man of peace and romance. The drunken bolide had looked into the depths of his nature and found something of warmth, colour, beauty to show forth to his greenhorns. It made sense that his wife had tolerated and stayed loyal to him for so long, because long ago, when he was young, he sang a love song to her.

In the summer holidays the Old Man sent congratulatory telegrams to David and Tom Selborne on their achievements in the external examinations. The boys returned for their last year at school in a blaze of glory.

Chapter 12

The Honours List on the wall of the large schoolroom showed their names, Sedgewick and Selborne, one above the other, shining in new gold paint.

'We've made it,' said Tom, but, when they passed the board, they looked up to reassure themselves they had not been dreaming.

Mr. Horn and Mr. Conway beamed with satisfaction. David's grade in art was a fluke. He had never drawn anything that showed the least animation or vigour, but the art mistress, who visited two afternoons a week, gave him an informal prize of a large drawing book in blue hard covers with tissues between the pages. He had never before been given such an expensive present. He did not deserve it, but the lady had seen him as vulnerable, in need of nourishment. He responded with enthusiasm, suckled, drew and drew for her pleasure and filled the book with stiff and spiritless creations. It did not matter. All she wanted was for him to use what she could give.

The Old Man descended the steps from his house and stood for a few moments under the covered way. Then he clapped his hands for attention and crooked his finger at the nearest boy. 'Find Sedgewick,' he ordered.

David expected the worst, but, to his surprise, received a sixpenny bit, smooth as satin. Apparently wishing to make amends, put his house in order, the Old Man showered young Sedgewick with favours. He gave him a ticket in the stand to watch a cup tie at Elm Park. 'Give them a cheer for me,' he said. When David took over as accompanist for school prayers, and played wrong notes, and muddled the pointing of the psalm, he took the boy gently to one side and told him to change the set hymn or chant whenever he found it too difficult. David's favourite substitute was *Oft in danger, oft in woe* which had no sharps or flats.

In November the Old Man suffered a haemorrhage and went to bed. When he rallied he sent for David. The boy, trembling at the thought of misdemeanours, climbed the steps into the house. His nurse had left the Old Man washed and comfortable, relaxed and propped with pillows. His great bulk, within the immaculate sheets, bolstered the bedding. The splotched hands lay prone upon the white over-lap of the sheet.

'My boy,' he said, 'do you see the monitor's badges on the table by the medicines?'

There they were, two silver brooches the size of shillings.

'I want you to take them and wear them.'

David picked up the badges.

'Now you may go.'

'Yes, sir. Thank-you, sir.'

The boy saluted and left.

Silver-tongued at last, the Old Man, by this quick transaction more appropriate to the study than to the death bed, consolidated the peace between himself and the boy. In December, at the Masonic Hospital, he died.

At the Old Man's funeral in St. Edmund's, David sang from Faure's *Requiem*.

Pie Jesu, Domine, dona eis requiem; dona eis requiem sempiternam.

Like the andante movement of Beethoven's Fourth Piano Concerto, David entered with a sad, slow song, *piano cantabile*. The Old Man replied *forte sempre staccato*, faded into *diminuendo*, and fell, eventually, into silence.

The grey ashlar mansion house, like a castle, stood on the highest level of the park. From it, the parkland sloped down and away into the separate valleys of the two rivers, the Thames to the north, the Kennet to the south. The mansion house survived only as a tea-house and changing rooms for teams playing cricket and football in the park. At the foot of the southern slopes, Sivier's boys played the last of the autumn term house football. A monitor refereed.

Mr. Conway, the duty master, had nothing to do but keep order. He walked over to where David, half reading, half watching the game, stood under the bare trees.

'What are you reading?' asked Mr. Conway.

'*Jude the Obscure*,' David said.

When Thomas Hardy died, David read an article about him and Tess in an old copy of *London Illustrated News* lying around in the schoolroom. The very title *Tess of the D'Urbervilles*, and the short account of her tragedy, motivated him to read the book. He had followed Tess through all her troubles to the shades of Stonehenge. For his birthday, Aunt Annie had given him *Jude the Obscure*. The noose of Jude's tragedy was tightening around him.

'The war of the flesh and the spirit,' Mr. Conway said.

'Sir?'

'That is what Hardy said his book was about. The eternal struggle. Jude, you see, wished to lead the intellectual life, but was drawn away by the charms of Arabella. It is one of the great themes of literature. You get the same opposing forces in *The Tempest*. Caliban brutish, animal and earthbound. Ariel intellectual, pure spirit. Life is conflict. We are all involved in some sort of struggle. Most of us survive. Jude did not.'

David, lulled into a false sense of security by favours received in the last few months, did not identify himself as involved in the common fight for survival, and could only guess at the full meaning of Jude's tragedy. Intimations of future conflict, simmering within him, were no more than as bubbles at the surface of fertile, primeval mud. His main concern was for Mr. Conway. There had been no official announcement, but everyone knew that he would not be returning in the New Year.

'Why are you leaving, sir?' David asked.

'I'm getting married,' said Mr. Conway, and felt obliged to explain his domestic necessity. 'You see, my wife and I will want to live together. There are no married quarters at Sivier's.'

'I'm sorry you're going, sir.'

'I'm sorry, too, in many ways.'

'If you became Headmaster you could stay.'

Mr. Conway laughed. 'That would be impossible,' he said.

'Why, sir?'

'I could not leapfrog Mr. Horn. You must see that.'

'You ought to be a Headmaster, sir.'

'Perhaps I will one day. I would like my own school.' Mr. Conway hesitated, then added 'What will you do when you leave next year?'

'I would like to write, sir.'

Mr. Conway looked thoughtful, as though confronted with a problem. 'You have the sensitivity,' he said. 'but I worry about your style. Don't be tempted into long, involved sentences. Keep your constructions simple. Try not to force an artificial style.'

David knew what he meant.

Mr. Conway accepted, with regret, that his pupils could only react sentimentally to literature. They had no experience of the passions which drive men into tragedy and error. With some boys, their puppy love would develop, in maturity, into a greater depth of understanding. He figured that Sedgewick might be one such boy. Knowing something of his background, he guessed that its complexities might explain the boy's failure at self-expression. It probably explained the lad's present silence. He put an arm round David's shoulder. 'Good luck,' he said, and returned to the touchline to watch the last of the football.

David felt a sort of love for Mr. Conway. Like Diana and his mother, the English master was at the roots of his life, tapping the earth's resources for him. He did not want to be cut off.

The North American tornado is called a twister. Its eye is dark and blind, its vortex random and volatile. It swings right and left, spins in circles, roars its head off and tears the ground. It uproots trees and houses, sucks up people, kills and dumps them miles from home.

Came the high wind to Sivier's. Mr. Tudor, an Old Boy of the school, left a successful business career in the City to become the new Head-master. He started a new dynasty. The Old Man is dead. Long live the Old Man. In March he bustled in on a wind of change and turned everything upside down. Winnie was blown to kingdom come. White table cloths floated down and covered the refectory tables. 'There are more things to school than passing exams,' said the new Head, and, being of a practical rather than academic disposition, he revived the school rifle club, ripped up one side of the gravel play area for allotments, declared the lawn no longer holy ground and used it for PT and cricket nets. An old Surrey player came once a week to coach. There were trips to the business world. Sir Alan Cobham dropped out of the clouds and whirled a party round his flying circus. A photographer blew in and took pictures of everything and everybody from every possible angle.

This bluff, amiable, social man, with a young wife, and a son and daughter at school, engaged an attractive young nurse to assist as Matron. Boarders, six at a time, took tea with the family in the drawing room on Sundays. Social graces became part of the curriculum. For an hour after prep the buttery became a dance hall. Masters and girlfriends, the pretty nurse, Mr. and Mrs. Tudor and their children mingled with boarders and danced to a gramophone. Tom and David, each with two left feet, hung on the wall.

In a year of change at Sivier's, Mr. Tudor was not the only freshman. The new, pink faced English master, fair and spectacled, and with a high shouldered, hunched look, like an American footballer padded for combat, had a straight-from-college enthusiasm, rubbed David like a new shoe, and covered his essays with bloody, red ink words. He told him to stop reading Thomas Hardy.

St. Edmund's changed its vicar. The new padre, a tough rugby player from Leeds, had no scrum cuddling when signing the Visitors Book. His tenor boosted the choir. David, from his top position in the adjoining stall, listened as he led the congregation in hymns and psalms. In the pulpit he showed his power. The church filled to overflowing every Sunday, like Easter Day. His sermons failed with Mr. Horn and Tom Selborne, but finally won David for Jesus.

David, like his friend, had only one more term at Sivier's. He soon learned that the monkey tricks he practised for Mr. Porter no longer found favour with the new regime. He could pass exams, but nothing he sowed in the new allotments came to fruition. In the carpentry shop he planed and chiselled until he found himself knee-deep in sawdust and shavings. His halving joints and dovetails fell apart. When he fired a rifle he closed the wrong eye. He and Tom had not the qualities demanded by the new order. At the tea party Mr. Tudor saw them clumsy and silent. When it came to the appointment of a new Head Boy they were passed over. The lot fell on their junior, who shone with buoyant personality and good looks, tufty blond hair and a ready smile which turned up at the corners of his mouth. Tom and David looked dead pan, dead as dodos, their flying days over.

While the new Head Boy ate spare sausages and bacon at one end of the buttery, the Headmaster, at the other end, laughed and joked with his wife and his staff eating breakfast at the other. They played golf together, practised their swings on the lawn and, at table, told each other tall stories. The dining-room rang with laughter.

David and Tom, out of touch with this brave new world, were shunted, with two other academics, into the vacant San to study, and forgotten. Every morning, left to their own devices without supervision, gossip took over. There was always something to chatter about; the new Head, his young wife, their daughter, the pretty nurse, the reforms, their grievances; jazz, films, cricket and girls, girls, girls. Small talk relieved the monotony of quadratics, graphs and French irregular verbs. In the upheaval of the high wind, they were left uprooted, buried in books.

Gawkish in other respects, Tom Selborne stroked a cricket ball with the grace of Frank Woolley, and captained the cricket eleven. David, chosen wicket-keeper, tested with fast deliveries by Mr. Horn, failed to read the movement off the seam. Extras piled up in school games. In the team photo, the keeper looked as though he should not have been there. Mr. Horn fixed him with his eagle eye, scared him with harsh words and kicked him out. The man of science had found the boy uncultivable, like a lump of clay, stepped on him and made him worse.

David defied the new English master and continued to read Thomas Hardy. For the new Elocution Prize he recited, besides the set pieces – Kipling's *If* and Newbolt's *Vitai Lampada* – the Dorset poet's *Tess's Lament* as the poem of his choice. He and his friend walked off with most of the sixth form prizes, and, for the Founder's Evensong at the end of the school year, took over the brass eagle lectern at St. Edmund's and read the lessons. Tom read from Ecclesiasticus – 'Let us now praise famous men' – and David from Corinthians with St. Paul's vision of pure love.

Mr. Tudor, like a builder modernising an interesting but dilapidated old house, cutting out worm eaten timbers, taking out partition walls, discovered he has smothered the garden with rubble, and attempted to rescue one of the plants. He summoned David to his study. 'What do you want to do when you leave school?' he asked.

'I want to be a journalist,' David said.

'There's no future in it for you,' the Headmaster declared. 'If editors paid by the yard there might be, but they don't. They like copy to be short and to the point. No long sentences, and no big words that no one knows the meaning of.'

Charged and found guilty, the boy looked downcast.

'Are you still reading Thomas Hardy?'

'Yes, sir.'

'I thought so. He likes long words and sentences, and he's an old misery, like you are. You make a good pair. If you're not careful you'll end up with a maggot inside you.'

Mr. Tudor lit a cigarette. 'There's this friend of mine,' he went on. 'He's an Old Boy. We were here at the School together. He's a surveyor. Just started up in practise and looking for a youngster to train. I thought of you and Selborne. Would you be interested?'

The freemason had friends at every corner who helped him set things in motion. He liked to juggle a few balls in the air. The two boys had become part of his act.

David had only the vaguest notions of a surveyor's job. He had not considered it and could not answer.

'You and Selborne are both well suited. You're both good at maths. Surveying involves a lot of that. Triangulation. Measuring distances and angles. That sort of thing.'

David brightened, glad to know that Mr. Tudor saw him as suitable for something, even though it was not journalism.

'Well, do you want an interview or not?'

'I'd like to try it, sir. Thank-you, sir.'

'Right then. That's settled. I'll arrange it and let you know. It's Mr. Castle. He'll give you all the details.'

Uncle Dick, worrying about Aunt Annie at the time, did not like the idea of the boy being a pen-pusher. He wanted him, like Andrew, in the rag and bone yard. In the end, however, he was persuaded to let David go for interview.

Mr. Castle's office, in a block at a busy cross roads where a policeman was always on duty, was noisy with trams clanging all day from three directions. David climbed two flights of stairs and, while he waited, sweated nervously in school uniform, and watched the sparks fly through the second floor windows.

The shorthand typist showed him in.

'Come and sit down, my boy,' said Mr. Castle, and offered the hot seat on the opposite side of his table. A lady sat on his right, with her back to the window. 'This is my wife,' he said.

'I feel I already know you,' Mrs. Castle said, and explained that she had seen him in the choir, coming down the aisle in St. Edmund's. She wore no hat, but the sun from behind gave her a sort of halo. Rich, auburn hair enclosed her face like the long, curved petals of a flower. Her eyes shone. She wore a cool, cream linen dress, square at the neck.

'You enjoy singing, don't you? I could tell.'

David noticed the wide mouth, relaxed and mobile, and the frailty of her body, light as air. 'My voice is breaking,' he said. wishing her to know he was growing into a man.

'Mr. Tudor has told me all about you,' Mr. Castle said in a quiet, good-natured voice.

The remark did nothing for David's confidence. What could the Headmaster have told him? He looked down, and blushed with self-doubt.

Mr. Castle relaxed in his revolving chair. Though slightly built, he emanated power. Hair sprouted strongly from ears, eyebrows and nose, but grew sparcely on the high, narrow dome of his head. The mouth was a crack, the nose strong above a high upper lip. The face broadened at the chin into a heavily folded lantern jaw. The deep chest, a barrel where one might have expected a ferkin, gave him an ape-like look. In the war, at a training camp, a giant gave him a rough house and punctured his lung. He had developed his thorax with deep breathing exercises.

'Don't worry,' Mrs. Castle said. 'There's really nothing to worry about.'

David, noting her reassuring glance, wanted to work for her, not him. She had a spirituality, as though she might be able to live without breathing.

Mr. Castle lit a cigarette from a packet of Gold Flake on the desk, and inhaled deeply. 'Mr. Tudor tells me you would like to be a journalist,' he said, and exhaled the smoke with his words, then coughed juicily and swallowed his rheum.

'Yes, sir,' David said. and wondered what else the Headmaster had told him.

'Well, you'll get plenty of opportunity to write here. Survey reports, sale particulars, advertisements and things like that. I'm a great believer in written records. Have you heard of Kai Lung?'

'No, sir.'

'He was a Chinese philosopher famous for his epigrams. Do you know what an epigram is?'

David defined an epigram.

'Good,' beamed Mr. Castle, signalling that the youngster had gone up in his estimation. 'Kai Lung said that the strongest memory is weaker than the faintest ink. If you write something down, you don't need to memorise it.'

Mrs. Castle had read, in the school magazine, David's account of the aeroplane trip with Sir Alan Cobham. 'I enjoyed reading it,' she said. 'It was very good.'

David welcomed the praise, but did not mention all the excisions and amendments made by Mr. Tudor to his original effort.

Mr. Castle tapped the desk with a gold pencil and explained that office hours were 9.00 am to 5.45 pm every day except Saturday when work finished at one o'clock. There would be an hour for lunch. Wages would be fifteen shillings a week to start. Prospects were good if David worked hard. Was that alright? Were there any questions?

There were none that David could think of, so Mr. Castle said he would let him know after he had seen Selborne.

As scholars, the two boys were neck and neck, but Tom Selborne, fluent essayist and stroke player, was in all other respects an ungainly hobbledehoy with unruly black hair and magnifying glass spectacles. David, more a little Lord Fauntleroy, was the lady's choice. She had seen his frailty, his vulnerability, his dreamy brown eyes, and told her husband that he was the one.

Tom Selborne stayed at the school as a pupil teacher.

George and Andrew suddenly fell out with the uncles over a small insurance which Nell had paid for out of her meagre resources. The uncles wanted most of it for funeral expenses. George did not agree. It was all or nothing, he said, a matter of principle. The uncles had the lot. George and Andrew left them, joined forces and shared the middle bedroom of another terrace house in Broken Brow.

The rats were slowly driving Aunt Annie into the grave. Neither of the uncles wanted David after the row with his brothers. That left Mr. Tudor with a problem. He could not send the lad out into the world with nowhere to live, and needed time to arrange something, so he sent David, with the nurse and his two children for a holiday with his parents who had a potato farm on the Sussex Downs above Rottingdean.

The old grandad met them at Brighton station and took them in a broken down Ford to the farm. The house, not much more than a hut on a hill of the open downland, had three bedrooms. The nurse and her charges crowded into the larger of the two spare bedrooms. David had the other. Every morning they broke their backs sacking potatoes, then old Mrs. Tudor packed them a picnic, and they marched over the Downs to the sea. Terry, the little boy, was too small to walk all the way, so the other three took turns to push him in a wheelchair over the chalk. All the while, Elizabeth, oval faced, wide eyed, and with long, dark hair, a little younger than David, chattered, laughed, asked questions. He, among strangers once more, anxious for the future, and insecure, retreated, like a young cub to its hole, out of the eye of the sun.

On the last day of the holiday, the weather was damp and chilly, and the four, in only their bathing gear, sat huddled together under towels against the sea wall. The nurse had a letter she could not leave alone, but kept pulling it out of her handbag and reading it. Her affair with young Mr. Jackson was well known. Everyone saw them in a love game when they danced together in the Buttery.

Elizabeth, impatient to share the excitements of the letter, could not contain her curiosity. 'How is Jacko?' she asked.

'He's not Jacko. His name is John. He's very well, thanks.'

The nurse, dark, silent, small featured and pretty, shivered with the others. The inner warmth of romantic love gave her no glow. The formal politeness of her reply showed her reluctance to be too intimate with her employer's daughter. They were good friends, but there was too great an age gap for them to be confidantes.

'Why didn't he come?' Elizabeth asked.

'He couldn't manage it. He had to go home to see his parents.'

Elizabeth expressed disappointment.

'I'm cold,' complained Terry, a pale faced, miserable child wriggling under a towel.

'We all are,' said Nurse.

'Come on, David, cuddle up and keep me warm,' Elizabeth urged.

David, on the outside of the group, next to Elizabeth, knew, deep down, that he should have claimed the closeness for himself, without being asked. He could not trust his natural inclinations, but edged nearer and touched her thigh, her ankle. It did not satisfy.

'Don't be shy,' Elizabeth said. 'Put your arm round me. I won't bite.'

David obeyed, but his arm, like a scarf placed lightly on the shoulders, communicated nothing.

'Have you any sisters?' asked Nurse.

'No. Just three brothers,' David said.

'Fancy having three like him. How awful.' Elizabeth teased her small brother and poked him in the ribs.

Terry pulled a face, prodded his sister and disturbed the towels.

'Now look what you've done,' Elizabeth said. She covered herself again, pretended to shiver and pressed closer to David. 'Would you have liked a sister?' she asked.

'Yes, very much,' David said.

'You can have her,' Terry said, and pointed his head at Elizabeth.

'And I would have liked an elder brother. Not this little shrimp,' Elizabeth declared.

'There you are, David, you've got a sister,' Nurse said.

'And good riddance,' said Terry, tightening up under the towel. 'I'm fed up with sitting here. I'm cold. Let's go home.'

'Stop whining,' said Elizabeth, 'We haven't had our swim. It's our last day, We can't go until we've had a swim.'

'I really think we ought to go,' said Nurse. 'It won't be any fun bathing. It's so cold.'

'I like swimming in the rain.' declared Elizabeth. 'It will warm us up. Who's coming?'

David felt her plump warmth against his body.

'No thank-you,' Nurse said.

'I'm not going in,' said Terry, and hugged himself under the towels.

'Come on, you babies,' pleaded Elizabeth.

'No, really,' said Nurse.

'No,' shouted Terry. 'How many more times?'

'What about you, David? Will you keep me company?'

'Yes, I'll come,' David said, glad to be asked, and wanting to please her and prove himself an elder brother.

Elizabeth jumped up and pulled the towels off Terry and Nurse.

'Oh, really!' exclaimed Nurse, annoyed.

'Pig!' shouted Terry.

'Come on, then,' said Elizabeth, and grabbed David's hand and pulled him up. Her shapely body looked fully formed inside her black swim suit.

David and Elizabeth ran hand-in-hand to the sea. David was growing fast. Elizabeth, with her long, lovely legs, looked tall. Her dark hair floated on the breeze, and, when they braved the surging waves, it fell almost to the water.

'Ooh! It's cold,' she said.

They loosed hands. Elizabeth hugged herself, then feathered the foam before plunging breathlessly and stroking forward into unbroken water. David followed. They laughed, turned on their backs, pushed each other with their feet, and laughed again when they missed. Afterwards, they swam seriously, showing off to each other, going out farther than either had intended. Eventually, on the turn, they came together, side by side, and struck out for the beach. In the shallow surf, holding hands once more, they dived into the breakers and came up streaming, yelling, laughing, the blood racing, tingling with warmth. David, washed and glowing, felt baptized, spiritually awakened, a new man.

'I've had enough,' Elizabeth decided.

They raced back to the others. Elizabeth snatched the big towel and exposed Terry and the nurse. The little boy grizzled. Nurse reached for her handbag and pacified him with chocolate. She shared the rest with David and Elizabeth.

David bustled to dress. Elizabeth stood statuesque, munching her chocolate. Like an animal, indifferent to weather, with only a towel about her shoulders, she looked warm and relaxed. She gazed into the distance, her expression thoughtful and sad, as though, in her day dream, she saw the future laid out before her.

'Come on, Elizabeth,' Nurse said petulantly. 'Don't just stand there. We're cold. Let's hurry up and go.'

She sprang to life and dressed quickly under the shelter of her towel. Her hair was limp and wet. She piled it up and wound the red towel into a turban. David stared, overcome with admiration. The impromptu headgear emphasised the glow of her oval face, its beauty and mystery.

Oh who will o'er the Downs with me...

They sang as they marched over the wet chalk to the farm.

In the evening they packed to go home. David picked up *Our Mutual Friend*, which he was in the middle of reading, and took it into the living room to put it back on the shelves.

'Have you finished it?' asked old Mrs. Tudor.

'No,' said David.

'Take it,' she said. 'Have it for a keepsake.'

Did she know how memorable the holiday would be for him? All evening Elizabeth filled his mind. He could never forget she had drawn him to her, and how they had run hand-in-hand to the sea. Her image kept him awake, then invaded his dream. Trainbearer, he lifted her hair into the wind until it flowed like a stream. Searching for the end of that dark mane, he distanced himself from her until she was out of sight. Trailing her hair, circumventing the earth, he returned to where she stood in the pool of the sun. He ran to catch and hold her. She dissolved in the sweat of his dream.